# Fearless

Priscilla West

# Chapter One

## RUN

Vicious scrapes covered my arms and legs. Pain throbbed steadily in my left cheek. Dull shockwaves pounded against the inside of my skull like someone repeatedly hitting my brain with a hammer. But worst of all, my eyes stung.

The tears threatened to fall, and I couldn't stop them. It was all so out of my control. All of it. The whole situation.

Everything was broken.

As my rock star boyfriend, Jax, leaned his chest against my back on the rumbling motorcycle, his soft, irregular breaths blowing against my ear, I knew nothing would ever be the same after tonight. If only we could rewind everything, to go back to that beautiful night in Las Vegas when it seemed like our world was unshakable.

I reluctantly brushed my cheek with the back of my hand, sweeping away the tears along with my hopes.

*We can't go back.* Not now. Not after what had happened.

My mind flashed back to how that ruthless biker gang, the Reapers, spit on Jax while he laid on the ground, broken and bloodied. They were led by Darrel, Jax's father—the monster who had beaten Jax as a child so many years ago, leaving him scarred, on the outside and the inside. I couldn't begin to imagine what it would be like to grow up with an abusive parent. To be small and helpless against the one adult who was supposed to love and protect you. He was the reason Jax walled himself off from everyone. He was the reason Jax holed himself off in his room, the Fortress of Solitude, escaping from the world through writing music.

And after all these years apart, *he* had beaten Jax again.

My hand tightened around the throttle as my sorrow boiled into anger. White-knuckled with my teeth clenched, I struggled to contain the storm brewing inside my chest until I couldn't anymore. Liquid fury rushed through my veins. They hurt him. They hurt Jax.

No one was going to hurt the man I loved and get away with it.

No, this wasn't fucking over yet.

In the driver seat, ready to go, I secured Jax's arms around my waist and raised the flaming bottle above my head.

"What are you doing?" Jax managed. His voice lacked the strength I'd grown accustomed to over the course of the tour, and I could barely hear him over the rumbling of the motorcycle.

My heart breaking for him, I lifted his bruised hand to my mouth and kissed it tenderly. "Burning away the past."

My fingers gripped the bottle hard. With the burning blouse sleeve hanging out the top beginning to singe my hand, I cocked my arm and heaved the bottle at full strength toward the house.

The bottle spun wildly, the flame at its tip lighting up the darkness as it ascended into the night sky. For a brief moment time stood still. All the anger. All the frustration. All the pain disappeared—eclipsed by one beautiful image—a jagged orange streak suspended above a row of rusty trailers stitched together like segments of a decomposed centipede.

That squalid hovel had been Jax's home, once. A house full of demons. He'd brought me to this place to show me his pain, to share with me the ugly scars he'd hidden from everyone else around him. It meant so much to me. It meant more than I imagined anything could.

Silhouetted against the blackness, the bottle flipped end over end as it began to descend, ushering a surreal silence in its wake.

The sound of my own heart pounded in my ears as an electric numbness washed over my body. My eyes widened in anticipation as the bottle fell toward its target.

This was it. The moment we fought back.

With a crash, the bottle struck a tree branch belonging to a gnarled cypress overhanging the driveway. Glass and alcohol exploded in a shower of fire, raining tiny orange-red comets onto the grass and asphalt below, shattering the stillness.

The street erupted into fast-moving chaos. Liquid flames sizzled out into the lawn, igniting the dry California grass. Fire crackled around Darrel's Cadillac and the bikes nearby, sending tendrils of hazy smoke into the air.

My stomach knotted with sudden, spiraling fear.

*Oh God. What have I done?*

I'd been stupid for boyfriends before. I'd done things I shouldn't have. But I'd never done anything like this.

Jax's mouth was open. His half-swollen eyes were wide. Dancing red-orange flames reflected off his dark irises. I tried to read the emotions I saw in the hard lines on his sculpted face, but his eyes were somewhere else.

Then, something charred and acrid stung my nostrils. My heart pounding, I shot a glance at Darrel's Cadillac parked in the driveway and saw the tires melting into the asphalt, bubbling up clouds of black smoke.

My limbs froze as I stared with horror at the growing inferno.

Through the haze, something shifted. The sound of rusty hinges creaking pierced through the crackling fire.

When I realized the source, my heart raced faster.

*The door to Darrel's trailer.*

"What the fuck?" A deep voice cried out. "Hey, boss, the bikes are on fire!"

I couldn't make out through the smoke who was talking, but then an unmistakable second voice boomed above the first one. "I'm gonna get that little punk!" Darrel growled. "And his bitch girlfriend, too!"

The situation hit me in full force. Darrel and his gang had let us go. We'd been free to leave, wounded with our tails between our legs, but free nonetheless. But now, after what I just did . . . A series of sobering realizations bombarded me in a sudden, sickening rush: Could I drive this motorcycle? Did I even remember how to get us out of here? *What the hell was I thinking?*

My stomach coiled viciously. I wanted to vomit.

*We might not live through tonight. And it's all my fault.*

The smoke rose in black plumes, burning my nose as I breathed in, making me gag, but I managed to stop myself from heaving.

Then I saw where the flames had spread, and my eyes widened in horror. Crackling at the underside of the black

Cadillac—Darrel's car—not far from the gas tank, the flames licked against metal.

"Hang on!" I cried to Jax frantically. "I'm getting us out of here!"

Jax moaned a wordless reply and I twisted the throttle. The engine growled in response, sending the bike speeding along the asphalt. We shifted precariously from side to side, Jax's weight on the back throwing the bike off-balance. Heart pounding against my ribcage, I turned left at the stop sign, hoping to god it was the way out.

Behind us, the Reapers shouted to one another.

"Get a fucking hose!" one bellowed.

"Our goddamn bikes!" another shouted.

As I turned the next corner, their voices began to fade. A feeling of thankfulness slipped into my chest, momentarily placating the fear and anxiety that had lodged there.

We were out. We were going to make it.

Suddenly, the ground shook beneath us.

BOOM!

What sounded like a missile exploding thundered somewhere from behind us. My grip on the handlebar jolted.

*The gas tank of the Cadillac.*

The bike careened off course toward the side of the street. The wrecked car I'd seen earlier stood directly in our path.

Screaming, I yanked the handle and jerked us back to the road—narrowly avoiding a head-on collision, but knocking off the right rear-view mirror in the process.

I righted the bike, managing to go straight ahead for the next few blocks without crashing. Barely. I wanted to stop, but I couldn't. I knew they'd be after us. I needed to get us as far away from this place as possible.

The cold wind whipped my hair wildly and raised goosebumps on my skin. I briefly clasped my hand over Jax's hand around my waist, ensuring he was holding onto me. His arms squeezed against my sides weakly.

"Stay with me, Jax," I cried. "Just stay here with me."

My mouth felt like I'd been eating cotton balls. Fear gripped my insides. The orange glow of the streetlights shimmered above us as I turned onto a four-lane road.

"Jax?" I shouted out. "Is anyone following us? Can you see anyone?"

Behind me, Jax moved slowly. After a few seconds, he called back: "No. No one. Not that I can see, anyway . . ."

The Reapers were probably busy putting out the fire, giving us the head start we so desperately needed. As the sign for the freeway approached, I quickly turned onto the ramp, hoping the extra speed would lose them for good.

I pushed the throttle higher, propelling us toward the traffic on I-5. The cars whizzed by like bullets, leaving a draft in their wake that teetered the bike dangerously. Too scared to go faster, I found myself in the right lane, being passed in a blur by the traffic around me.

BEEEEEP!

A sharp horn blast from behind nearly made me jump off the bike. As I checked my mirror, I expected to see Darrel preparing to ram us. Instead, there was a teenage kid in a Honda Civic, passing us on the left like we were standing still.

"Learn to ride, asshole!" the kid called back, his mop-top head momentarily jutting out from the driver side window.

"What's going on?" Jax said, sounding dazed. "Why are you going . . . going so slow?"

I checked the speedometer, expecting to see the gauge at highway speed, but it was barely reaching forty. "It's hard to keep control of the bike! I don't want to go any faster than I'm going right now!"

"Faster is easier. More momentum . . . just . . . try faster. You'll see. Trust me."

I wanted to object, but feeling stuck between a rock and a hard place, I mentally crossed my fingers and pushed the throttle higher.

The engine growled as the bike picked up speed. Oncoming wind whipped my hair back and forced me to squint my eyes. The wobbling began to fade, and within moments, the bike seemed to stabilize.

Suddenly, a car lurched into our lane, cutting the bike off, and stopping my heart.

Clenching the handlebars in a death grip, I swerved, feeling the bike tilt beneath me.

"Fuck!" I screamed, zipping through a space between a car and a pickup truck.

When the offending car passed us, I broke into a cold sweat. But judging by the "I <3 LA" license plate, it didn't seem like one of the Reapers. Just an asshole L.A. driver.

*Jesus. That prick could have killed us.*

As I tried to calm my frantic heartbeat, I saw something beautiful just a little further ahead: six lanes of middle-of-the-night, empty, black Los Angeles freeway, just one blue

Ford pickup truck away. A surge of adrenaline coursed through me as I pushed the bike past eighty.

"Eat my dust!" I cried to the truck, releasing newly pent-up frustration toward California drivers. The driver of the pickup flashed his middle finger at me as I watched him fade out of sight in the rear-view mirror. The further we went, the clearer it was getting that wherever the Reapers were, they hadn't followed us onto the highway. Their bikes were huge—and *loud*.

Before I could relax, I felt Jax's grip around my waist loosen.

"Keep talking to me, Jax," I called back to him nervously.

His arms squeezed tight again. His fingers were tense this time, almost clenched. *From pain?* I didn't know.

Finally, his words came out. "Just . . . get me home, okay? Take me home."

I shot a quick glance back at him with narrowed eyes. "But you're hurt!" I cried.

"I'm fine. Had worse nights than this." His voice sounded like he was gritting his teeth.

"Jax, I think we should take you to—"

Red-and-blue lights flashed in the mirrors, and a siren blast echoed through the night.

*Oh god. No.* It was the worst case scenario.

"Shit! The cops are right behind us!" I shouted to Jax.

I'd been so scared about the Reapers that I hadn't even thought about the police. But it all made sense. I'd committed arson and destroyed property. I was a criminal. A fugitive from justice.

But I couldn't go to jail. Not for this. Not now.

I pushed the throttle.

As the bike picked up speed, Jax grabbed my waist sharply. "No!" he shouted, more forceful than I'd heard him since his last interaction with Darrel. "Pull over to the side. Let me handle it."

Behind us, the sirens were close and getting closer. My head swam with terror. The world was collapsing around me, and there was nothing I could do about it.

Tears streamed down my eyes as I started pulling over to the side of the road.

*This is it. End of the line.*

My career was over, and so was Jax's. We'd be humiliated, disgraced in the tabloids. I'd have to move back in with my parents . . . if they'd even take me in after finding out their daughter was an arsonist. I'd get one phone call. I tried to remember Kristen's number. Could she bail me out, hire a lawyer? It would be mortifying to call her and Vincent, but they were my best hope.

As I slowed down, the sirens got impossibly loud and close behind me. Then a pair of cop cars sped past us like we didn't even exist. They zoomed off, chasing a red sports car further down the road.

I took a long, deep breath, trying not to sob with relief. *What was I thinking?* The Reapers were a biker gang. They'd probably committed worse crimes than arson. They probably wouldn't call the cops on us even if their lives depended on it—at least, I hoped not.

Releasing a breath of relief, I revved the engine. Feeling a little more confident on the motorcycle now, I found myself zipping deftly to pass cars and trucks. As I steered the bike off the interstate, I started to recognize the area near the Roman, where the bus was parked.

And that left just one obstacle: the guard at the gate. I breathed deep, trying to keep my emotions under control as I slowed down to stop at the security booth.

"Beautiful ride," the guard said, looking the motorcycle over from top to bottom. He was muscular, broad-shouldered, and his bronze nametag said "Gus." I tried to keep my hands from shaking as we idled in front of him. "You're from the Hitchcocks, right?" he asked.

"That's right," I said. *Good thing he recognized us.* I didn't have any ID on me, and I had no idea if Jax had brought his.

"Geez," Gus said, taking a long look over Jax in the dark. "He looks like he had a long night."

I gulped. "He, had a couple drinks too many," I said, surprising myself with the sudden lie. "Fell down on the sidewalk."

Gus shot Jax a knowing smirk. "I hear that, man," he said sympathetically. "I used to be a bouncer."

Even though it seemed like the coast was clear, I couldn't shake the prickle at the back of my neck. "Has anyone come around looking for us?"

Gus's face suddenly looked concerned. "Looking for you? Like who?"

I froze. "No one. Forget I said it. Everything's okay here, though?"

Gus bent out of the security booth, using his flashlight to peer at Jax and me carefully. In the harsh glow, I could already see angry bruises forming on Jax's face.

"Are you sure you two are okay? He looks pretty beat up."

Jax put his hands over his face, shielding his eyes from the flashlight's glare. "We're fine! Stop shining that thing in my goddamn face, will you?"

My eyes widened. I hadn't expected Jax to be so coherent. Or so angry. "I'm sorry," I cut in quickly. "It's like I said, he's been a little overserved. It's been hard enough just getting him back home, so if you could do us a huge favor and just . . . don't tell anyone we were here. We just want to get some sleep."

Gus's face softened, and he shook his head with a smile. "I guess you're only young once," he said, a conspiratorial gleam in his eye. "Don't worry, your secret's safe with me. Have a good night, you two."

Numb from the shock of the night, all I could do was nod and smile weakly.

Gus pressed a button on the panel in front of him, and the gates opened wide. "Make sure he drinks plenty of water," he chuckled. "The morning after's a bitch!"

I looked back to give him a half-hearted grin, then turned to see where we were going.

It was only as we saw the bus across the lot that I finally felt my sense of impending doom lift. There it was, in all its glory: a triple-decker touring band's dream, complete with rooftop hot tub. When we drove behind the bus and saw the black-and-gold storage trailer, I realized I could finally feel my hands again.

I'd been taking things a moment at a time since getting on the bike, but the enormity of what I'd done hit me with full force as my breathing started to return to normal. *God, it could have been so much worse.* If the flames from the bottle hadn't reached the Reapers' bikes or the car . . .

Shaking my head at the grim thought, I pulled the bike into the trailer. So far, the Reapers were nowhere to be found. They hadn't followed us from what I could tell, and even if they had, there was security around the area, and the bus was like a triple-decker tank with its bullet-proof windows. We were in safe territory.

"Almost there, Jax," I said softly as I got off the bike. "We just have to get back on the bus."

*The bus.* I swallowed hard. *Shit.* The rest of the band. They were probably waiting for us, and they weren't going to let us get away with a couple of easy cracks about falling on a sidewalk.

I draped Jax's arm around my shoulder. "Let me help you."

He bristled, trying to move away. "I'm okay. Don't worry about me."

I could tell he was covering up pain. But then again, after the night we'd had, he'd have to be. I bit my lip and helped him limp toward the bus door.

My stomach was doing backflips as I tried to figure out what to say to Sky, Chewie, and Kev that could possibly explain Jax's injuries. Already, his face swelled with bruises. How could I face them and tell them what happened? I'd been helpless, defeated. We both had. The band would feel guilty, sad, maybe deceived—I had no idea which.

Bracing for the worst, I turned the key and the door popped open.

Inside, there was nothing but total darkness. I reached up for a light switch, worrying about what to say. With a wince, I held my breath and flipped the switch for the auxiliary lights.

There was a mess of clothes on the ground, a bag of weed on the table, and Chewie's ghost detector lying on the couch, but no one was around.

"Where is everyone?" I said, confused.

I followed my nose to find Chewie's half-smoked blunt on the living room table, next to a folded note:

*Party at Lizzie Boham's house. If you two horndogs ever get back from wherever you went to do the nasty, meet us there.*
*- The Chewster*

In the front room, Jax was still looking for the rest of the band. "Sky? Chewie?" he said.

"Over here," I called to him.

Jax walked stiffly into the living room.

I held up Chewie's note. "Look at this. They're all gone. They're not even here. It's . . . it's . . ."

Jax scanned over the note, and one corner of his lip turned up wryly. It wasn't exactly a smile, but it was something.

After all the terrible, traumatic things that had happened tonight, something had gone right.

A sound started from the back of my throat, and I held it back for a moment, expecting sobs. Instead, when I opened my mouth, a laugh came out—a sad, relieved, quaking laugh that shook my entire body.

*It's going to be okay. We're not going to die. I'm not going to jail. We're going to survive.*

I doubled over, unable to stop laughing. Too overwhelmed to speak, I gasped in big lungfuls of air, tears rolling down my cheeks as pained laughter poured from me. I was alive, and so was Jax—and for the moment, that was all I needed.

# Chapter Two

## DAMAGED

As I struggled to control my laughter and tears, Jax broke into a raspy, hacking cough. The sound came from deep in his lungs, and he leaned against the couch as he struggled to catch his breath.

My laughter cut off mid-breath as I snapped back to reality. "Jax!" I cried.

"I'm fine," he answered. He straightened with a grimace, wheezing in air before letting out another, smaller cough.

I narrowed my eyes in concern. As I scanned his body for wounds, he tilted his head away from my gaze. A patch of crimson glinted from beneath his hair.

"Stay right there," I said, pulse racing. "Actually, no. Sit down on the couch."

As he lowered himself gingerly onto the couch, pushing the ghost detector aside as he did so, I snapped on the bright overhead lights. Jax groaned and squinted, his hand reaching up to shield his face from the glare, while I stepped toward the couch to take a closer look.

What I saw made my stomach turn.

Blood caked over the side of his scalp, crusting and darkened at the edges.

I swallowed, trying not to let Jax see how scared I was. The terrifying memory flashed behind my eyes: Darrel slamming the butt of a pistol against the back of Jax's head, leaving him laid out on the street. I'd never seen someone beaten so badly before. I couldn't imagine the pain he must be in. Or how badly his whole body might be damaged.

In a fit of irrationality, I quickly snapped the light off again, as if blanketing the wound in darkness would somehow take it back to the way it was before I'd seen how bad it was in full light. I had to fight hard against my instinct to take him to the hospital right away. From the way he responded to the guard, I knew Jax was already irritable. If I suggested he needed serious care before even taking a closer look, he'd get stubborn—and that was the last thing either of us needed when the stakes were so high.

"I'll be right back," I said, careful to keep my voice from trembling.

My heart beat anxiously and my hands shook as I ran hot water from the bathroom tap onto a clean washcloth, then brought it back out to Jax.

I turned the light back on before approaching him. He hadn't moved a muscle, and was sitting tiredly on the couch.

"I need to clean this out a little bit," I said softly. "I'm going to try not to hurt you . . . but it looks bad. I can't promise anything."

"Give me that," he said as he grabbed for the washcloth.

I pulled the cloth out of his reach, not surprised by his response. Jax was trying to be tough, but the wound was on his head. He couldn't possibly see it well enough to clean it properly. "Let me. Really," I offered, trying to figure out a way to assuage my worries without wounding his pride. "You helped me clean up when those guys chased us onto the bus, remember? I'm just returning the favor."

His mouth stretched to a thin line, as though he was formulating an objection. But then he closed his eyes and nodded, his body relaxing into the couch.

I forced a small smile past my apprehension. Raising the warm washcloth to his head, I pressed it against the clotted blood on his hair and started to wipe away rust-colored streaks.

When I gently increased the pressure, he flinched.

My touch lightened instantly. "Sorry."

He remained silent, staring at the opposite wall.

After a few moments, I managed to clean most of the surface of his hair. I now needed to see what the actual wound on his scalp looked like. Steeling myself against the possibility of finding something horrible, I parted the black strands of his hair carefully. My eyes darted back and forth between the wound and Jax's restrained expression.

There was a gash. A small one, though. More like a cut. Blood had stopped flowing from the opening, and every wipe of the washcloth sent fresh relief through me. It had made a mess, but there was no way he needed stitches.

I released a deep breath. *Thank god.* He'd been beaten, but he wasn't broken.

"There," I said, gently wiping the last of the blood away. "That looks a bit better."

Jax let out a low grunt. "Thanks."

The head wound looked like the worst of it, but I knew it wasn't the only place where he'd been hit. "Now . . . can you take off your shirt for me? I need to take a look underneath."

"Later," he said dismissively.

I set the washcloth down on the side table and went to get the first aid kit I'd remembered was stored in a cupboard near the bar. "Better to patch you up now than to wait for morning," I called back.

His eyes closed as he took a long, deep breath. When he opened them again, his voice was soft and low. "Fine, I'll do it. For you."

I squeezed his hand, quietly accepting the significance of his words. Part of his irritability and defensiveness came from the physical pain, but a larger part came from how vulnerable he was feeling at the moment. And as difficult as it was for him, he was willing to lower his guard, to be vulnerable, for me. "Thank you."

Together, we slowly lifted his shirt off. He winced hard as he moved his shoulders, stiffly sliding his muscular arms out. I looked at Jax's torso, naked as the cloth peeled away, and suddenly felt like all the air had been sucked out of me.

An angry bruise, red, green and black, radiated in an irregular circle from his side, a Rorschach blot of pain and suffering. Raw and shiny, the dark splotch stretched halfway across his body.

I'd never seen a bruise so big. I suddenly felt like I'd been the one kicked in the gut.

Jax saw the expression on my face and looked down. He tried to shift his torso away so I couldn't see the bruise, but it was too late.

I sank down near him to take a closer look. Circles within circles patterned his side. This was clearly a lot worse than a normal bruise—it was the result of heavy boots repeatedly kicking at the same unprotected area. It was a bruise with bruises of its own.

"It's really not as bad as it looks," he said quickly, casually sliding his arm over to cover the discolored skin.

I held my hand near a black-purple spot toward the center. I probed the tender skin as gently as I could. "Does this hurt?" I asked, looking into his eyes.

He swallowed stiffly, his body tensing. "Not much."

He was beginning to put up his guard again. I wanted him to see a doctor—and soon. "I need to take you to the hospital to get you checked out."

"I'm *fine*." His tone was low, with a forceful edge.

I looked at him sitting there on the couch: his hair hanging in limp tangles damp from the washcloth, his body battered.

"Jax, I'm not trying to pressure you, but you don't seem fine." I took his hand into mine and gave it a soft squeeze.

Darkness clouded his face as he pulled his hand away. "Dammit, Riley," he snarled. "I told you I'm fine. I'm not going to spend the night in some hospital just so you can feel better."

The blood drained from my face. Suddenly, my hands were icy cold. I knew Jax was tired, hurt, and upset, but I didn't know why he'd make it so personal when I'd done everything I could to help him. I opened my mouth to reply, but nothing came out.

As my eyes began to sting with tears, Jax looked away, a pained expression on his face.

"Fuck." His voice was much quieter now. "I'm . . . sorry. I know you're trying to help. I just . . . I fucking hate hospitals. Can we drop this for tonight?"

I wanted to say yes—but even more than that, I wanted Jax to be okay.

He looked at me tenderly and gave my shoulder a soft squeeze. "I'm fine. Really. I know it looks bad, but it's really not that bad. It's just a bruise. I've had much worse. Trust me."

The sincerity in his voice momentarily broke through my worry, making me realize that I'd been shaking. I'd just had the craziest night of my entire life with multiple close calls for both me and Jax. Was I overreacting? The blood on his head had looked so much worse than it turned out to be. Maybe he had a point.

I touched his side again as a sanity check.

He exhaled. "I didn't say it doesn't hurt. It does, but I'm saying it's not serious. At least it's not, unless you keep poking it."

"Okay," I said finally. "But if it gets worse—"

"I'll call a doctor." His eyes, no longer dull and glazed, had a renewed depth I realized I'd been missing. "I promise."

Looking into his warm gaze, I felt tense muscles I didn't even know I had starting to relax. My shoulders loosened, and I exhaled all at once. The relief was palpable. The crisis was over, at least for tonight.

"Let's go upstairs to rest," he said.

We made our way up the stairs one slow step at a time. As we entered his room and laid down, I shook my head, trying to make sense of everything. I still couldn't believe the night we'd had. It felt like a terrible dream.

Memories flashed across my skull like a slideshow. The flickering firelight, the street lit by a Molotov cocktail—one that I'd thrown. Darrel's gravelly voice calling me a *little bitch*, the Reapers kicking Jax with sounds that still echoed faintly in my mind . . . how long would it take me to get the images out of my head?

"You okay?" Jax said, a look of concern on his face as he laid next to me.

"Yeah," I replied, trying to smile. "I'm fine. Just a little tired, that's all."

He touched my cheek softly before flicking off the light. I nestled in against the warmth of his body, taking care not to press on his bruise.

Within minutes, he was snoring softly. I laid awake, listening to his breath. I'd almost lost Jax tonight . . . and in the end, we'd both been lucky to make it out as unscathed as we did. I shivered, unable to stop seeing Darrel's angry face every time I closed my eyes. He was Jax's *dad*—and he only wanted to hurt his son. The injustice of it struck me to my very core. And now, with Jax resting up in his bed, it was like there'd been no real consequences. He seemed unperturbed, at least for now, but I wasn't so sure. In my experience, life didn't work that way: when you did something that big, you couldn't just walk away without feeling the effects one way or another.

I curled my hand around Jax's hip. With time and rest, our aching bodies would recover. But I'd seen the pain in

Jax's eyes—would time and rest be enough to heal that kind of hurt?

# Chapter Three

## THE MORNING AFTER

The next thing I knew, I was sitting up in bed, coughing.

Heavy smoke spread thickly throughout our room, choking me. The smell of burning rubber assaulted my nose.

*Fire!*

I flung out my hand to wake Jax—but my hand only brushed an empty spot. He was gone!

Panic raced through my body. Where was he? I knew he wouldn't leave me in danger unless . . . he was too hurt to help me.

I jolted out of bed, tortured by visions of Jax hurt and trapped by the fire that raged somewhere down below. He could be worse than hurt, he could be *dead.* My heart seized with terror. I had to find him, had to get to him somehow, no matter what. Even if that meant going into the fire myself.

I opened the door, and a heart-stopping BOOM twisted up from below. A heavy hot gust of air hit my face. I was falling . . . Jax!

My eyes shot open. I stared at the tapestry-lined ceiling of Jax's bedroom, panting. Sunlight poured into the room.

My heart thumped in my chest, and I took a moment to catch my breath.

It had just been a nightmare. The most horrible kind— the kind that felt real.

I'd thought the Reapers had come and torched the bus and that the worst had happened.

I thought I'd lost Jax.

I rested the back of my hand against my damp forehead and slowly closed my eyes again, allowing a smooth stream of air to escape from my lips. We weren't in danger. We were safe. No Reapers had come looking for us in the night. How could they? They didn't know where we were; they'd been too busy dealing with the fire on their bikes to follow us.

I reached over, searching for the comfort of Jax's body, but my hand brushed a cool emptiness on the mattress where his body should have been.

"Jax?" I turned over to find him gone. Confused, I sat up and clutched the sheet to my breast.

Scenes from my nightmare flashed before my eyes, and a terrible sense of foreboding swept through me. I was suddenly haunted by the thought of losing Jax, for real this time. *Where is he?*

I grabbed a pair of jeans off the floor and hopped into them, cursing loudly when I banged my shin against the open closet door. I shrugged a t-shirt over my head, paused to consider putting on shoes, decided against it, and flew out the door.

Out on the landing, I hesitated. Should I check upstairs first?

A harsh clang burst from below.

I started, then raced down the stairs, skipping the last few steps and landing with an impact that sent tremors through the bus's steel floor. Four heads snapped up to look at me.

*Jax.*

He was sitting on the couch next to Sky and Kev, while Chewie crouched on the floor, paused in the middle of wiping up a wet puddle with a rag. The awful-smelling liquid came from a two foot tall bong that glistened damply from being knocked over.

I heaved a sigh of relief at the unexpected normalcy. The flat screen TV was on, showing footage from what looked like the concert last night. A half empty pizza box lay on the table, surrounded by random piles of scribbled-up note paper.

The strong sunlight filtering through the windows meant it was at least noon already. *I slept ten hours?* It was little wonder: after the terrors of last night, I'd been exhausted. From the state of the living area, it looked like the rest of the band had been up for a while.

"Whoa," Chewie said, "You got here fast. It's like ringing a bell." He picked up the bong and righted it. "Give me a minute and I'll get this warmed up for you."

"Uh, no, thanks," I replied, feeling a little awkward about my grand entrance over what was apparently just some weed smoke.

Sky bounded up from her seat and grabbed my hands, pulling me down on the couch between her and Jax.

She touched my scraped cheek gently, her brown eyes wide. "Hey, Jax wasn't kidding. You did save him."

My heart skipped at her words. Had Jax told them what happened last night? My eyes darted over to him. He was holding an ice pack to the side of his face, but the bruising around his eyes was now minimal. His olive skin was a little paler than usual, but overall he looked far better than he did last night. A half smile even played across his lips.

"Man," Kev said with a laugh, "And I thought the party *we* crashed last night was wild."

I blinked, then mentally kicked myself for being so stupid. Of course he hadn't told them, or at least not the whole truth. But that left me unsure about what to say until I found out exactly what he *had* said.

The faces around me were eager for my response. I hesitated, then said, "Ours wasn't much of a party."

"Yeah, Jax told us," Sky said. "It's happened a couple times before. He beats a lot of people at pool."

Chewie smirked. "Not all of them take it so well."

I snapped my head up and peered at Jax. So that was his story.

Sky looked at me sympathetically. All I could think was, *you don't know the half of it.*

"You should've seen Riley whipping her cue around, Bruce Lee style." Jax shook his head. "I never saw anything like it." He leaned over and kissed my unbruised cheek. "My baby is such a badass."

I feigned a smile, confused and slightly embarrassed that Jax's made-up story was beginning to border on parody. But judging from the band's bored expressions, they'd heard crazier.

"Too bad you guys didn't come with us," Sky said, a huge grin suddenly streaking across her face as she changed the subject. "We partied at Lizzie Boham's house! It was so wild."

If they'd gone to Lizzie Boham's house, then they must have been hanging with the A-list Hollywood crowd. And I'd read stories about the excessive, booze- and drug-fueled parties at Boham's Beverly Hills mansion. "Really?" I asked, glad to be changing the topic. "Did you crash it?"

Kev shook his head emphatically. "She was at the gig and dropped us invites. I think she was disappointed Jax didn't show." He made a wry face. "Figures."

Chewie laughed. "No, man, she got over it. Once I rolled her a tasty blunt, she forgot about him real good."

Jax reached over, wincing a little, and poked Chewie's shoulder playfully. "Watch out—if you keep hanging with her you might make the tabloids."

The more Jax acted like nothing had happened, the more concerned I felt about him. Burning down your childhood home wasn't the kind of thing you could walk away from without some permanent scarring.

"Nah," Chewie said before taking a giant rip of the bong. He exhaled a skunky cloud of smoke towards the ceiling. "I can do that by myself. But if she wants to tag along, I won't stop her."

Everyone laughed, and I snuck another look at Jax. Just a glance at his handsome,bruised face made my heart beat a little faster. He was smiling along with the rest of the band, laughing like it was any other day.

His lightheartedness, bordering almost on cheerful, struck me as unusual. Then again, I remembered how I'd laughed right after we'd gotten back. Maybe Jax was just now having the same rush of excited relief I'd had before.

Jax's hand darted out with lightning-quick reflexes as he grabbed the remote from Kev and turned up the volume on the TV. "This stuff came out really good." The camera panned around the stage, stopping momentarily to highlight each of the band members, then zoomed in close to Jax's face. The Jax on TV held the microphone close to his lips, his eyes squeezed shut, with his voice rising in passionate abandon.

Sky laughed and pointed at the screen. "You look like you're about to give that microphone a blowjob."

I whipped my head around to look at Jax, expecting to see him scowling with irritation. Instead, Jax just grinned. "Nah, that's not my style."

I managed a small smile. A real one, this time. But I was also burning to talk to Jax alone, to see how he was doing. Unfortunately, the band looked comfortably camped out, watching the footage.

"We're just lucky they filmed this before you went and got your head bashed in," Kev observed. "That wouldn't have looked so good."

Jax just shrugged and we all kept watching the TV. After about ten minutes though, he pressed pause. "You guys don't have to keep watching if you don't want to." He turned to Sky. "Didn't you say you wanted to hit the beach?"

She nodded. "Yeah, I could finish watching it later. I want to soak up as much sun as I can while I'm here. Anyone with me?"

"Me," Kev said, a grin lighting up his boyish face. "I could use some waves."

Chewie stood up too and stuck his drumstick in his back pocket. "Yeah, and I could check out the babes. I like me some California girls." He began humming the Beach Boys song under his breath.

Sky turned to me and Jax. "What about you two?"

Jax shook his head. "No, I want to finish watching this."

"And I'm still tired from last night," I chimed in, relieved that Jax had found a way for us to be alone.

The band horsed around as they got their swim stuff together, with Chewie taking the time to rip another couple massive hits on the bong. Then they left the bus, earnestly and loudly debating whether to hit Venice Beach or Santa Monica.

It was just the two of us now.

I curled my legs up on the couch and shifted around to look carefully at Jax. He'd set the ice pack down, and the lightheartedness in his face had switched to concern.

He touched my cheek, his eyes resting on the scrape I'd gotten last night. "Are you okay?" he asked, his voice filled with urgency. "I was so messed up last night, I didn't even check you out."

"I'm fine," I protested as Jax picked up my hand and looked at it closely. "I want to ask about you."

"This is a burn," he said, ignoring my words and pointing to the small red spot where the molotov cocktail had singed my skin. He got up and grabbed the first aid kit from the table.

"It's nothing," I said, knowing that my minor scrapes and bruises were nothing to fuss about. But Jax just opened the kit anyway and took out a small bandage. His brow furrowed as he secured it over my tiny burn.

"Are you hurt anywhere else?" he asked when he finished, his eyes filled with concern.

My heart swelled with a sudden rush of affection. How could he be so hurt himself, and still worry over me?

"I'm *fine*," I insisted gently. "But what about you? Should we call the doctor?"

A flash of emotion clouded his face, but then it was gone. "I'm fine too. Actually, I feel a lot better."

I peered at him, wanting to take his word for it, but the memory of his gigantic bruise left me still doubtful. "Are you sure about that? Last night—" I cut myself off, not wanting to force Jax to relive the memories.

"I'm sure," he replied, his voice firm. I knew that tone. When he sounded like that, there was no arguing with him. I would have to respect that he knew his own body—if he said he was fine, then it must really not be as bad as it looked.

He picked up the remote and turned the TV back on. We sat in silence. After a minute, I glanced at his face. Now that he'd stopped worrying about me, his expression was almost cheerful again as he watched the concert footage. I wanted to ask him more, to find out how he was really feeling about what had happened to him last night, but something in his face made me hesitate. It seemed like he was determined to not let the trauma of last night upset him. But how could he not be upset, when his own dad . . . I shuddered.

An image of Chewie bashing on the drums zoomed up on the TV. Jax stared at the screen intently, then jotted some words down in the notebook that he had balanced on the armrest of the couch.

"What are you writing?" I asked, wanting to say something, get him talking to me. Maybe I could find out something that way.

He finished scribbling his sentence, picked up the remote, and paused the TV. Excitement made his eyes glitter.

"The filmmaker wants us to review the raw footage from last night, tell her what we love and hate. If I get this done quick she can start editing, blast out a film, and we capitalize on the goodwill from this tour."

He sounded so happy. "Oh," I said, "That's good for you guys then. Is it a lot of work?"

He grabbed my legs and swung them in his lap. "No, or I'd ask the rest of the band to help. But I got this."

He smiled at me, and began rubbing my bare feet. His strong hands squeezed my arches, and my toes curled with pleasure. He was being so sweet, so positive—I guess of all the ways I might have thought he'd be acting this morning, *happy* was the last that came to mind. But here he was, right before my eyes, smiling at me.

"It's nice to see you in a great mood today," I said carefully.

He nodded as he massaged each of my toes, one by one. "It's all coming together. With the band, with you—" he broke off to give me another kiss. "You know you're a kickass, beautiful girlfriend."

I hesitated for a moment before squeezing him back affectionately. Still no mention of Darrel, of any of it—maybe it was just too hard to talk about.

I ran a finger through his hair and tugged at the ends. "You sound like you've got it made." My voice was gently inquiring.

"Uh huh. Especially after I play the show tonight. It's gonna be wild."

"Oh." I blinked rapidly. That was right. They had one more show at the Roman.

Somehow, it didn't seem right that he would go on stage, not after all he'd been through. What if he made himself worse, by spending the massive amount of energy he needed to perform? And no matter what he said, he had to be in pain.

"For some reason I thought that might get rescheduled," I said, keeping my voice light.

Jax stopped rubbing my left foot and raised his eyebrows. "What? It's been sold out for I don't know how long."

"But theoretically it could be done though, right?" I asked. "No one loses out. The tickets just get automatically transferred to the new date."

"Yeah, and everyone's disappointed."

"But it happens all the time. I can't tell you how many shows I've had rescheduled on me."

He snorted and resumed his caresses, this time focusing on my calves. His inky hair partially hid his face, but I could see his lips curved wryly. "C'mon, I bet you weren't too thrilled when they did that."

"Yeah," I admitted, "But I'm just saying it could be done. With probably just a few phone calls."

He tucked his hair behind an ear and gave me a stubborn look. "You make it sound easy, but I don't think that's how it works."

I bit my lip. Even if he was well enough not to go the hospital, he still might not be ready for any taxing physical stuff. An image of Jax's violent beating flashed through my mind, and I repressed a shiver at the memory.

I traced a feather soft finger across his shoulder blade. "No one would blame you if you took some time off to heal."

He shook his head. "I'd blame me. I'm not gonna let down my fans, or my band, or you."

"Jax, you wouldn't let me down—"

"This is going to be the best show of the whole freakin' tour," he continued. "I'm not going to cancel." He gave me a piercing, haunted look. "I need this."

His warm, calloused hand gripped mine. I could sense wound up energy coiled deep inside his body, and somehow I knew this was about more than just being a dedicated musician. I placed my hand over his heart and gazed into his intense, dark eyes. He *needed* to play tonight—and let out all the emotion he'd been holding back.

I took a long slow breath. I was still worried about him, but Jax knew better than I what was good for him. If this was what he needed to heal, then I wasn't going to stand in the way.

"Alright, go get your rock on." I kissed him softly on the lips. "I know you'll be amazing."

He stroked my hair and smiled contentedly. "Pepper, you're one in a million."

We stayed cuddled up as he picked up the remote and restarted the footage. I kept my hand in his, enjoying the closeness of his touch.

It seemed odd, that after all that had happened to us the other night, we could just go back to our lives like we'd never been through hell. So far, it was all working out better than I could've expected—the Reapers were off our tail, no cops had hassled us, and the band hadn't even been upset by what happened, thanks to Jax's cover story.

Jax furrowed his brows in concentration as a new camera angle popped up on the TV, and a reddish scrape along his jaw shone in contrast with his olive skin. He'd been hurt so much in the past, but now everything seemed to be working in his favor, thank god. He deserved it more than anyone.

After the nightmare of last night, it seemed like everything was going to be all right after all.

# Chapter Four

## THE SHOW MUST GO ON

Before I knew it, I was standing in the same sidestage spot I had watched from just the day before, waiting with trepidation as the venue finished filling up with fans hoping for the show of their lives. The energy in the building seemed to have its own pulse. Everyone wanted The Hitchcocks to come on stage and begin the show. Everyone wanted Jax. The Roman was rocking, and the show hadn't even started yet.

While the crowd was humming with anticipation, I was simply nervous. My mind buzzed with exhaustion as I tried to fight back my worries. Jax said he would be fine—and there was nothing left for me to do but just trust that he was right. Still, I repeated a mantra that contained every hope I'd had since I had gone to sleep the previous night.

*It's going to be okay. Jax is going to be okay.*

Finally, the lights went dim. The crowd erupted as The Hitchcocks filtered onto the stage, Jax last of all. As soon as the crowd caught sight of him, they somehow screamed even louder. Jax was right. These people would have been *very* disappointed if he had cancelled. I just had to hope he would make it through the performance in one piece.

He stalked forward to the edge of the stage, took the microphone off its stand, and froze, standing there in leather pants and a black t-shirt that stretched around his shoulders and chest like a statue of rock god perfection. The stage lights came on. Chewie hit his sticks together with four rhythmic clacks, Jax sprang into motion, and the band began to play.

Like a taut bow finally released, the show was on, and the crowd was in a frenzy as they sang along with their hero. Several women toward the front, dressed in matching Hitchcocks t-shirts, screamed in unison before flashing the stage. Kev gave a sly grin to Chewie, who nodded back. Sky rolled her eyes, but Jax seemed not to notice.

Even through my exhaustion, I could see that for this set, he was *in it*. There was nothing else. It was obvious why he needed this. Between the music and the energy of the crowd, there was no time to think or worry. About his dad. About his demons. About anything.

As the band settled into the show, I watched as Jax moved around the stage as energetically as ever, seeming totally unaffected by his injuries. He was in full Jax Effect mode, and every woman in the building—myself included— was falling under his spell. With every song, my worries about the safety of Jax performing drained away more and more.

This was his element—and as I watched, I gave myself over to the energy of the band, unable to tear my eyes away from Jax. Somehow, the past twenty-four hours had changed something between us. Before, I had been trying to see past his stage persona to find the real him. But after sharing with me his true, traumatic past, I knew what fueled his passion for music, and what I was seeing on stage wasn't just an act for the crowd. It was about as close as Jax ever got to showing his true self to the world.

At least, as close as he got with anyone but me. We had something different.

The energy in The Roman continued to build as the band cruised through the first half of their set before coming to the set's first ballad. Sweating profusely from the performance, Jax took a drink of water and pulled out a stool to sit on as he typically did for this part of the show. While I couldn't see his face from my vantage, I could see the suddenly serious expressions on the faces of his fans, and it felt like everyone's mood had shifted. Now that they had rocked, it was time to get raw.

Jax looked around at the audience as he took a seat on the stool, microphone in hand. He seemed to be even more emotionally invested in this song than normal. The way he slouched down after he sat, collecting himself, sent a stab of worry through me. Were his injuries beginning to affect him?

But then the band began to play and he sprang back into life, crooning through the first verse of the song. He came to the chorus.

> *And when you pick at scabs before*
> *they've healed you open up the door*
> *to feel like bleeding might be best today.*
> *You bare your secrets . . .*
> *alone.*

I had heard him sing this song many times, but this was the first time I had heard it and knew the secrets he was hiding, the scabs he was hoping would heal. Before last night, he had only ever opened up the door to those secrets to write them into his songs, but he wasn't alone anymore. He had me, and I was going to help him heal once and for all no matter what it took.

The intensity of my feelings as I watched him, glistening under the stage lights in front of adoring fans, scared the hell out of me. We had only known each other a few weeks, and yet the connection I felt with him was unlike anything I had ever experienced.

Was I losing my mind? Last night I had thrown a molotov cocktail and burned up a bunch of bikes belonging to a motorcycle gang. People were supposed to settle down as they aged, but with him I was feeling more out of control than I had ever been.

Still, I was crazy about him, and I couldn't shake that feeling. Even if life felt like it was spinning out of control, Jax made me feel more alive than I ever had before.

I shifted back and forth on my feet to the beat of the song as it built towards its climax. Even if the way I felt about Jax scared me, being with him was something I wanted. I knew he had demons he hadn't faced, and I knew it would be hard, but that didn't matter to me.

What mattered was the man who had trusted me enough to bring me to the heart of his trauma. After that, I knew he believed in me. And I believed in him.

Jax hopped up off the stool and wobbled as he went down to his knees for the end of the third verse. I hadn't seen him do this before, and even caught Sky send a questioning look over his way. She quickly wiped it from her face and returned her focus to the show. Jax kept singing, seemingly without problem, the volume of his voice rising as the music got louder for the last chorus.

He put his soul into it, clenching his free hand into a fist as he bent over, sat on his heels, and spat out the words inches from the fans in the front row. They ate it up and sang along with him, tears in their eyes and rolling down their cheeks. I blinked and realized I was crying along with them, the performance tugging at my frayed emotions. His music was so beautiful.

He reached the last line of the song. The lights went dark and the pyro kicked in, silhouetting Jax in an orange glow. Still on his knees, head back, he screamed the last note, his voice going through several levels of hell as he twisted and squeezed every ounce of pain he could from the song. Finally, his voice gave out, the music stopped, the final pyro flared, and he fell from his knees onto his back.

My heart stopped. Time stopped. Something was wrong.

The crowd cheered in the background like static from a radio station out of range. I waited for Jax to get up. A spotlight shone down on him as the last chord from Kev's guitar finally gave way to silence.

Jax's head lolled over to the side so that I could see his face. His eyes were closed, the lids almost snow white, a single strand of dark hair falling across them. His lips were faintly pink, almost blending in with the rest of his skin.

Now that I had a good look at him, I saw that his entire body was deathly pale. This was bad. Jax was not okay.

My stomach clenched in agony. A feeling of disoriented shock coursed through my body.

"Jax!" I screamed desperately.

I continued screaming his name at the top of my lungs and took a couple steps onto the stage before being hit in the shoulder and falling to the ground. I looked up and saw two medics rushing past me with a stretcher. My chest constricted painfully, like I was trying to breathe underwater.

Shivers went down my spine. Chaos erupted all around me. A flurry of bodies—including several fans who had been in the front row—were suddenly on stage and I lost sight of Jax. My heart crumpled up in my chest as I got up and tried desperately to elbow my way to him.

Was he okay? Would I ever get to talk to him again?

Nobody was moving and time slowed to a crawl and the night felt like it stretched into forever. Before I could reach him the medics had him on a stretcher and took him away in a haze.

I wiped the tears from my eyes and began following them. My fingers felt like ice.

# Chapter Five

## WAIT

I found the band backstage and we all hurried to get a cab, barely speaking to each other. Everyone was in shock, and we rode to the hospital in a grim silence. Once we got there, all we could do was wait.

Two hours later we were still waiting without any word from the doctors, and my nerves were ragged with tension. I paced up and down the ER waiting room, my hands clenched together behind my back. My mind had been taken hostage with worry, and I couldn't stop the image of his collapse from playing over and over again, torturing me.

With a sigh I threw myself down in the closest chair. Kev and Chewie were sitting across the room, talking quietly to each other. Sky sat next to her brother, flipping through a magazine, but she was going too fast to really be reading it.

A doctor came into the room, searching the faces of the tired people before looking down at the clipboard he was carrying. I started up in my chair, but slumped back down when he began talking to a middle aged woman sitting near the front desk.

Restless energy filled my body, and I tapped my feet nervously on the cheerless gray carpeted floor. An oppressive weight stuck hard in my chest. I'd handled this situation all wrong. I should've taken him to the hospital last night despite his resistance. The signs had all been there: the bruising, the paleness. Why hadn't I put two and two together?

*I'll never be able to forgive myself if something happens to him.*

I leapt to my feet, unable to bear sitting any longer, and began pacing again. My eyes lost focus as I stared down at the waiting room's ash gray carpet.

If I hadn't pushed him to open up to me, we never would have gone to his old house, never had that horrible ordeal with Darrel, and Jax would be healthy and whole right now.

I had been way too vulnerable after the shock of seeing Connor again, and in my desperation to stifle old, unwanted feelings, I'd tried reaching out to Jax. And stubbornly refused to back down when he told me he didn't want my help. In my misguided attempt to be supportive, I'd only proved how bad I was for him.

I bit my lip as choking sadness welled up inside me. My eyes began to sting with the threat of tears. I blinked rapidly, not willing to let them fall.

"Riley," a soft voice said.

I stopped pacing and turned around. Sky stood there, her arms crossed against her chest. Her eyes were anxious.

"Want to take a walk with me and go find some coffee?" she asked. "I can't stand this waiting around."

I gulped, trying to loosen the knot in my throat. "Yeah, I could use some too."

We made for the exit that led to the hallway. A sign painted on the wall pointed the way to a cafe, and we headed down that corridor.

"I can't believe this is happening," Sky said, her voice tinged with apprehension. "Jax has gotten into so many scrapes before and he's always been fine. What happened last night, Riley?"

Violent images of the previous night flashed before my eyes, and my stomach twisted. I was the only one who knew the truth. I wanted to tell Sky, but a part of me knew that Jax had kept it a secret for a reason. He would want me to stick to his cover story.

I took a shallow, shuddery breath. "The fight in the pool hall was worse than Jax made it seem. Those guys were really big and nasty, and he got pretty beat up. I wanted to take him to get checked out at the hospital but he refused to go. He said he was fine, and I believed him."

I closed my eyes briefly at the painful memory. "He looked alright. In the end I didn't think it was that bad. I don't know how I could've been so stupid."

I paused as we walked into the coffee shop. Coming after the hushed silence of the waiting room, the cafe was a jarring cacophony of human and machine made noises. The clamor seemed to echo the muddled state of my mind.

We ordered our coffee, and I fumbled in my purse to get the money to pay for both.

"Thanks." Sky held the cup up to her lips, but didn't take a sip. She looked at me with concern filling her large brown eyes.

When she spoke again her voice was quiet. "I think anyone would have made that mistake. Jax looked okay to me this morning, except for the bruises, and I've seen him with plenty of those over the years."

My fingers reflexively clenched on the warm coffee cup. I shook my head. "I should have been watching him closer."

Sky tugged at my sleeve and walked over to sit at one of the tables in the middle of the room. I followed and dropped into a chair facing her.

She took off the lid of her cup and blew on the hot liquid inside. "You're not a doctor, Riley," she said while looking at me from over the rim of the cup. "And it's pretty hard getting Jax to do anything he doesn't want to."

"Yeah, but still, I should have taken better care of him. I let him down."

Sudden tears made my vision blurry. My heart felt like it was getting squeezed in a vise. I only wanted to help Jax, but instead I'd hurt him. It was like living out my worst nightmare.

Her lips tightened in sympathy. She gave me a compassionate look, then reached out and patted my hand. "You know I've known him since we were like fifteen?"

I nodded, my fingers picking at the plastic lid of my coffee cup.

"You know what Jax was like back then? Stubborn. Pigheaded. Completely out of control." A warm smile tugged at her lips. "And totally awesome, of course."

I managed a small smile despite my nerves. Jax at fifteen must have been a trip.

"Well, he was really wild." She shook her head ruefully at the memory. "And I mean out of his mind reckless. He was always doing crazy, daredevil stuff. Sometimes it was fun, but sometimes it was real scary hanging out with him. Like one time when Jax decided that he wanted to subway surf."

My eyes widened. I remembered reading about that in the Village Voice. Thrillseekers climbing on top of subway trains as they hurtled through the tunnels, looking for the ultimate joyride. It was so crazy it seemed like an urban legend.

Sky took a sip of coffee before continuing. "There we were, waiting for the R train in Brooklyn real late at night, and I was so terrified I was shaking. He could have gotten seriously hurt, or worse, you know? But nothing I could say would talk him out of it."

A fragile smile turned up the corners of my mouth. "That sounds like the Jax I know."

"Yeah, right? He rode that train, and there was nothing I could do about it. And I knew he'd probably do it again, too. Or something worse."

I mused on her words for a moment. "Why do you think he did stuff like that?"

She sighed. "I wish I had an answer, but I don't. I wanted to know about his family and home and stuff, like maybe that had something to do with it, but he always stonewalled me. All he'd ever tell me about himself was that he's from California, and he hitchhiked to get to NYC. Eventually I just stopped asking."

My palms were slightly sweaty and I wiped them on my jeans. On some level, I'd always assumed that Sky knew at least part of Jax's history. They were almost like brother and sister; it was strange he'd shut her totally out.

I scooted my chair closer to hers. "I actually never heard how you two first met."

Sky smirked. "Well, that's Jax for you, Mr. Incommunicado. I was going out all the time and was hardly ever home. I was a sucker for live music, so I always hung around this all ages punk club slash art collective on the Lower East Side. Jax and I ran into each other at a hardcore show and hit it off when we found out we both loved Black Flag. We were pretty much inseparable after that."

"So then Jax stayed with you after you guys got to be friends?"

She shook her head regretfully. "No, even though that would've helped him out a lot. He was always scrounging for side jobs he could work under the table because he was underage. But my parents had enough of their own problems to want a random teenager staying at their townhouse. You know, the whole 'we married for money and status and now we're miserable' thing."

She put her elbow on the table and plopped her chin on her hand. A mischievous look settled onto her face. "I was really rebelling against them hard when I met Jax."

I gave her an encouraging smile. "I guess hanging out with him would be a good way to do it."

"If they only knew the half of what we got up to!" Sky said with a laugh, her eyes bright. She took another sip of coffee and leaned forward, her expression growing serious again. "But he was the wild one. Like I said, he didn't ever care about himself. It was like he lived for taking risks. And sometimes the stuff he did was super dangerous, like the subway surfing. I used to worry about him a lot."

"How did you deal with it?" I asked sympathetically.

Sky shrugged her narrow shoulders. "It was hard, because I was just a kid too. But I got lucky. One day we found these guitars tossed in the alley, and took them back to his place to jam. He lived in this one bedroom apartment he shared with a buddy from a restaurant he used to work at, and he slept on the couch. Tight quarters, but he was happy he had a place, and I liked to be anywhere that wasn't home.

"We didn't know anything about how to play, but Jax got completely absorbed in learning." She spread out her hands for emphasis. "I mean he spent every day playing until his fingers bled. But that was cool, because playing the guitar changed him a bit. He was still kind of a daredevil guy, but he stopped taking those risks that could've killed him."

"Wow," I said, feeling my lips curve upward. It was easy to picture Jax bent over his first guitar, doggedly picking out notes and chords until he got it just right. He must have felt so much triumph and pride every time he made a new breakthrough.

"So he found something better," I murmured.

"Yep. Music helped him." She paused, and looked at me with a serious expression. "But Riley, I want you to know something. You've helped him too."

I blinked my eyes. "I have?"

She nodded emphatically. "Yes. Because Jax has always had problems, has always been stubborn as hell. But when he's with you, he's happier than I've ever seen him." She paused to give me a sincere smile. "And it means a lot to me that you can do that for him."

My heart swelled as I took a deep, sudden breath. She was so kind. For the first time since Jax's collapse, I felt like I had a reason to be hopeful about us.

I smiled back at her warmly. A tear hovered at the edge of my eye, but this time it was a happy one. "It means a lot to hear you say that. Thank you."

Her eyes brightened at seeing me cheer up. "I just don't want you blaming yourself for things you can't control. Jax is changing for the better just because you're around." She laughed. "I mean he's still a stubborn pig, but he's a happy stubborn pig."

I laughed along with her, wholeheartedly this time. It felt good, like the knots in my belly were finally becoming untied.

I stood up and stretched. Giving her another smile, I said, "C'mon, let's go check up on our guy."

We walked back to the waiting room, which was still crowded with weary, worried people. When we got back over to where Kev and Chewie were sitting, they informed us that they hadn't heard anything yet. The guys were looking pretty nervous and frustrated too with all the waiting.

As the minutes ticked by, the more I fidgeted in my chair. I was able to remain sitting though, and for that I was grateful.

Then a doctor in a white coat came into the room, one that I recognized from earlier. My eye caught his, and he instantly strode towards me.

The doctor stopped short in front of our group. "You're here for Jax Trenton?"

"Yes," I gasped out. I looked at him desperately.

He cleared his throat and clasped his hands behind his back. "He's going to live."

# Chapter Six

## DOCTOR'S ORDERS

I saw Jax a few hours later. Exhausted eyes looked back at me from too-pale skin, but all in all, it could have been a lot worse. According to the best doctors in LA, Jax had been bleeding internally in his abdomen since the fight. The blood clotted at first, making him feel well enough to go on stage, but his energetic performance the night of the concert had ripped open the clot. The scary part was, if we'd have waited any longer than we had, there might not have been a recovery.

Guilt was tearing me apart. I told him that I should have tried harder to make him get checked out, but he waved me away and said it was his fault. I didn't know whether he was on some kind of drugs for his pain or if he was just tired from losing so much blood, but he seemed pretty out of it.

The nurse hurried us out after a few minutes and we were told we would be able to visit Jax again during regular afternoon visiting hours. With time to kill and nothing on my mind but Jax, I decided to go out and find him a get well soon gift.

A couple of cab rides and a trip to the Apple store later, I had a gift for Jax. Since it looked like he'd need to take it easy for a while, I'd looked for something that would provide a positive distraction. I even managed to find a drug store nearby so that I could wrap it for him. By the time I was finished putting the finishing touches on it, visiting hours had started.

As I entered Jax's room, I found him propped up on some pillows, staring at the wall with a sullen expression and a couple days of stubble on his cheeks. He had already gotten a little color back, but he still didn't really look like himself, lying there with an IV in his arm and wearing a hospital gown.

Still, he was alive, and the smile he flashed when he turned his gaze to me warmed me up.

"Hi Pepper," he said weakly, adjusting himself so he sat up a little straighter.

"I came back for you!" I chirped, trying to be as cheerful as possible.

He nodded and gave me a small smile. "I see that. Thanks."

A silence hung in the air for several seconds as I studied his face. He seemed to be staring off, trying to keep his eyes on me but unable to do so for any length of time. Something was weird about him.

I pulled his gift out from behind my back, hoping it would cheer him up. "I got you something," I said, keeping my voice bright.

His brown eyes opened wide and he took the gift from my hands. "What is it?"

I was happy to hear a little life in his voice. "Open it!"

Tearing open the paper, he revealed the iPad I had bought for him and turned it around in his hands. I had even managed to find some Hitchcocks stickers for the back to make it more personalized, and when he inspected them on the back he smiled.

"Thank you," he said quietly, turning so his gaze met mine. Even though his voice had livened up a bit, his eyes still seemed distant, like he was swimming to the surface just to talk to me. "This is perfect."

I nodded, even though his expression worried me. "You're welcome," I said, trying to keep things upbeat. "Turn it on! I loaded it up with a few surprises."

He obeyed as I leaned around to look over his shoulder. "See? I loaded it up with every Hitchcock movie I could find. So now you can watch them wherever."

"Wow," he said, looking back up at me, and I caught a glimmer of warmth in the dark depths of his eyes. "You really thought of everything. Thanks."

He arched his neck so that our faces were close and I leaned down to give him a kiss. Our lips locked tenderly, sending a warm feeling down my spine. I wanted desperately to curl up with him in his bed and be close to him. The intimacy of his touch, even if it was just a simple caress, was like nothing I'd felt with anyone before.

His lips lingered on mine before we broke off the kiss. I straightened up and gazed into his eyes, my mind racing with all the things I wanted to say to him. "Jax," I said softly, "I never want to lose you."

His dark brows, including his beautiful eyebrow scar, arched. "Lose me?"

My stomach twisted as the memory of his collapse flashed through my mind. "I know you didn't want to let your fans down, but you nearly died out there!"

"But I didn't," he said, his voice gruff. "And I won't let my fans down. Ever."

I nodded quickly and put my hand on his shoulder to reassure him. "I know, I know. But when I saw you fall over on stage, passed out and pale . . . and then some fans were up on the stage, crowding around and getting all hysterical. I didn't know if you were going to make it. It was scary! Maybe it would help to get some better security at concerts."

"Pepper, let's not talk about this," he said, exasperation heating up his voice. "It was a freak thing."

My throat caught slightly as I felt my emotions rising. His mood had changed so quickly. "But what about if your dad's bike gang tries to hurt you? The Reapers? If they found us, they'd want revenge, right? I don't know, it seems like some extra security can't hurt."

He shook his head. "I don't think the Reapers are coming after us, Riley. And even if they did, extra security at the concert won't help that, but it *will* make my fans feel less close to the band and that would suck."

I took a deep breath. He had a point about the fans. "Well, can't we figure out something? I almost lost you twice in the last few days, and that really scares me."

His eyes narrowed. "But I'm fine. Doc says my recovery should be no big deal, just a little rest. I'm sorry I scared you, but it's in the past now."

"What about security for the bus? We could talk to Reed and—"

"Pepper," Jax interrupted, his face hard. "This conversation is over."

I studied his face. He seemed so stubborn and moody— not that I could blame him, after what he'd been through. There was no getting through to him at this point. Defeated, I slumped my shoulders and looked around the room. Maybe I could talk to him again some other time about The Reapers. It just seemed like we had to do *something*.

"How do I get games on this thing?" Jax asked.

"What?"

He held up his new iPad. "Do you know how to download games?"

I shook my head, stunned by how quickly he had changed topics. "I guess you need to connect to the wifi around here. I don't know what that is."

He blinked and looked down at his device before looking back up at me. The distant look was back on his face. "Whatever. We can figure it out later."

I shrugged. "Okay. How about a movie?"

"Huh?"

"One of the movies I put on your iPad."

"Oh," he said, still distant. "Yeah. Let's do that. How about *Vertigo*?"

"Whatever you want," I answered. At this point I just wanted to keep the peace.

He started the movie up, and after grabbing a chair to sit next to him we watched it until we were interrupted by the other band members returning from lunch. As I watched him interact with the band, I couldn't help but feel a pang of worry. Something was up with him. Maybe it was painkillers, maybe it was what happened at the concert or with his dad, but something was up. And I knew now wasn't the time to push. At that moment, I felt like all I could do was hope he would heal as the days wore on.

# Chapter Seven

## ON THE ROAD

Jax was released from the hospital a day later. I had been hoping his mood would improve once he was out—he'd said he hated hospitals—but it didn't. Even when Reed called to tell us he'd booked one more gig, this time at a big outdoor festival, essentially extending the tour by two weeks, Jax seemed irritable and just shrugged.

The rest of the band had been overjoyed, though, and I emailed Palmer, asking him for some vacation time. There was no way I could make myself leave Jax now, not when he seemed to need me the most. But to my surprise, Palmer extended my job with the Hitchcocks, saying that I shouldn't leave until the job was truly finished. That meant I didn't even have to burn any vacation time.

I was relieved—but also for the first time, I found myself wondering about what really *would* happen after the tour wrapped up. Before the incident with Darrel, I hadn't thought about it much. Everything was going so well between me and Jax that I'd just been taking it one day at a time. But after almost losing him, I knew that he meant more to me than any guy I'd ever met.

Yet Jax's strange mood compelled me to keep my mouth shut, and not bother him with details when he was still struggling with whatever was troubling him. I wanted to focus on getting him better first—then I'd worry about us.

So we settled down to wait for the festival. After two days of hanging out on the bus, which was still parked at the

Roman, everyone was bouncing off the walls—and had noticed Jax's strange moodiness.

Luckily, Reed came through by putting together some promo work for the band to do. Some interviews, photo shoots, and the like. Not as exciting as playing a rock show, but it was something. And when Sky heard that we needed to head up to San Francisco for an interview, she had a brilliant idea: road trip.

A day later, we were driving up the Pacific Coast Highway, taking in the scenery.

"Pull in there! This looks like a good one!" Sky pointed toward a roadsign marked 'State Park-Beach Access.' Just beyond, the waves of Big Sur crashed onto a sandy expanse of shore.

From the front seat of the red rented convertible, Chewie tapped his sunglasses in acknowledgment. "You got it," he said, turning the wheel left. "One sunny Big Sur beach, coming right up."

Sky had been the one to propose taking the scenic route—and renting the convertible was all Chewie's idea. They said it was for a change of scenery, but the quiet glances back and forth told me everything I'd needed to know: they were as worried about Jax as I was, and wanted to get his mind off the disastrous show and its aftermath.

I looked next to me, where Jax was playing a game of Threes on the iPad, nervously flicking his finger back and forth over the screen. "Hey, check it out, Jax." I nudged his arm as Chewie drove slowly onto the park road. "It's gorgeous out there."

Outside, the scenery was pitch-perfect—but Jax's eyes were still fixed on his game. "It's a beach," he said, without looking up. "They're all the same, and we've already been to three today."

Sky and I shared a look: *What can you do?* It was par for the course on the trip so far. I'd given Jax the iPad to help bring him back into the world, but my plan had backfired. Instead, he was using it to check out completely. The trip up the Pacific Coast Highway was one of the most beautiful drives I'd ever seen, but whenever we passed a fabulous rock outcropping or a celebrity house, he was gritting his teeth, too wrapped up in the tablet to notice anything around him.

As Chewie parked, Kev put on his sunglasses. "Everyone out!" he said.

Sky climbed out of the back seat, her blonde hair blowing in the wind as her sandaled feet emerged onto the parking lot asphalt. "Ahhhhhhh!" she said with a dreamy sigh, stretching out her arms in the salt breeze. "God, I love California."

She looked back to Jax and me expectantly. I got out in a hurry, but he dragged behind, tablet still in hand.

I nervously considered asking him to leave the iPad behind. At first, I'd wanted to take his newfound tablet obsession as a compliment to my gift-giving skills: he clearly really liked the gadget I'd given him. But the more he'd played, the more it became clear he was irritated and withdrawn, his expression more compulsive than entertained. But how could I tell him to stop when I'd given him the gift in the first place?

"Hey, guys, babe with blue hair at six o'clock," Sky said, breaking me out of my reverie.

I swiveled around to see a park-uniformed woman with short, electric-blue hair walking backwards as she gestured toward a group of fifty-something tourists with binoculars. As she turned toward us, I saw that she was holding a large device connected to an antenna.

"Aw, man, this is perfect!" Chewie's voice was awed. "That's the Plasmatic XL, the best ghost detector ever made."

Kev squinted. "Isn't that the same one we have?"

"No, doofus," Chewie said, rolling his eyes. "We have the Plasmatic. That's the XL. And that has got to be the girl of my dreams."

*A ghost detector in a state park?* It seemed pretty unlikely to me. Sky, judging by her dismayed look, felt the same way.

Chewie, deep in conversation with Kev, didn't seem to notice either of us. "I'm going in, man, back me up."

"Always the wingman, never the wing." Kev chuckled, shaking his head as he followed Chewie toward the building marked 'Discovery Center,' which the tour group had just disappeared into. "Just remember to invite me to the wedding."

I looked back to Sky and Jax, uncertain whether we should go with them or walk down to the beach. If Jax had heard any of Chewie and Kev's conversation, he wasn't showing it. It was like there was a wall between him and the outside world and nothing was getting through. Sky looked to Jax, then toward the building, and frowned.

"Maybe we'd all better go in there and keep an eye on them," she said. "I've seen Chewie like this a couple times before, and he needs all the help he can get."

I nodded as Jax grunted his assent. "Sounds like a plan."

\*\*\*

The Discovery Center was a dark wood-stained building with large glass windows. When Sky, Jax and I walked in, we saw Chewie and Kev deep in conversation with the blue-haired woman, who stood underneath a display of posters full of birds and their eggs.

"Of course, conservation efforts have been quite—" the woman cut herself off as we approached, calling out, "Hello there! I'm Camille."

"Hi! Riley," I said, extending my hand as I marveled at the photos of vultures that lined the walls. With a nod to Chewie, I asked, "Find any ghosts yet?"

"Yeah," Sky said sardonically. "Careful with that thing or you'll summon the Stay-Puft Marshmallow Man."

Chewie's face contorted into a sheepish grin. "Ghosts?"

Sky squinted at him. "Um, yeah? Remember the ghost detector?"

"That's not a *ghost detector*," he said quickly, as if we were being ridiculous.

Kev grinned. "Yeah. You guys will believe anything. This is a. . ." He looked back to the woman. "What was it called again?"

Camille flashed a wide smile—she was beautiful, and it was clear that Chewie and Kev were hanging on her every word. "It's an advanced radio-frequency tracking system," she said, then turned to me with the device. "Do you want to hold it?"

I looked at the remote control-like gizmo in her hand, confused. "Wait. What are we supposed to be tracking, exactly?"

"The flock, of course!" Camille said, with a tone that clearly asked, *what are you, dense?*

Not wanting to sound ignorant, I just nodded awkwardly. "Of course!"

"If this is your first time at the center, it's your lucky day," she continued, her hands moving animatedly as she talked. "We've been tracking the Big Sur flock all day, and I'm about to go back to the bluffs. We're expecting to see three, four birds, maybe even more."

*Birdwatching?* It wasn't exactly my idea of a good time, but Chewie was rapt. "And you'll teach us how to use that thing?" he said excitedly, pointing to the 'ghost detector.'

She smiled. "That's right."

"I gotta huddle with my buddies for a second, here, okay?" Chewie turned back to us. Lowering his voice almost to a whisper, he said, "Guys, you've gotta go with me on this one."

Sky's nose crinkled. "I don't even know what this is all about," she said, sounding skeptical. "Birds, I guess?"

"I thought it was the girl," Kev said. "Or the ghosts. Which was it, again?"

Chewie shrugged, his shaggy hair bouncing around his face. "If we're lucky? Both."

Birds and binoculars weren't quite the thrills I'd expected on my rock tour assignment, but if it was to help Chewie?

I turned to Jax, hoping for some kind of reaction to the idea—positive or negative. "Jax? What do you say, do we go with or do we skip it?"

His tone was flat. "Whatever. It's better than more sand. Probably."

Maybe something was going to get through to Jax, but this wasn't it. I turned to Camille with an apologetic grimace.

"Follow me this way and we'll get started," she said, looking totally unflustered. I still felt a little embarrassed by Jax's antisocial behavior—and concerned about the emotions that could be causing it, especially since the convertible had left us with no privacy to talk about anything significant.

As we walked down the sidewalk away from the center, Camille held the radio tracker up. "How many of you have ever seen a California condor before, either in the wild or at the zoo?"

Everyone was quiet, except Sky, whose voice tentatively called out, "Didn't condors go extinct?"

Camille surprised me by nodding in response as she adjusted the antenna. "You're right, actually. They did go extinct in the wild—all the way back in 1986."

Sky looked confused. "But that means . . . "

"See?" Chewie said triumphantly. "I told you that thing was a ghost detector. Man, this is what I love about California."

"Condors aren't ghosts," Camille said, looking amused. "I said they went extinct in the wild. Twenty birds were left in captivity, and we've reintroduced their chicks—and their chicks—to the park and the areas beyond."

She moved the tracker antenna through the sky. From the cliffside, we could see rocks jutting from the water below and ancient trees clinging to the shore, but I didn't see any birds. "You kind of did bring them back from the dead, then, in a way," Sky said, sounding a little awed.

"Not from the dead. Just from the brink." Camille smiled as she slowly turned the antenna on its axis. Suddenly, she stopped and pointed. "There! Right over that curve. See him?"

Sky peered out, her hand shielding her brow. "See who?"

"Amigo! You can see his wings, he's heading straight toward us."

Squinting, I looked out toward the horizon until I made out a black shadow that grew bigger and bigger until an impressive wingspan fanned out over the beach below.

"Whoa, guys, check that out!" Chewie said excitedly. "I see him! Hey, Amigo, que pasa?"

Camille's voice called out to us. "Amigo's actually a very lucky bird. Not too long ago, we weren't even sure he was going to make it."

Kevin's brow furrowed as he tracked the condor through the sky. "Wow, what happened?"

Amigo swooped toward the beach as Camille handed the tracker to Chewie. "He got into a bad accident," she said. "He was recuperating for a very long time."

"You hear that, Jax? Sounds kinda like you." Chewie turned to Camille with the tracker in hand, practically skewering her with the antenna until she redirected it gently back toward the beach. "My buddy Jax here just got out of the hospital."

Jax looked up at Camille and Chewie for a long moment before letting out a grunt and looking back down.

Camille gave a concerned look to Chewie. "I'm glad you're feeling better," she said to Jax evenly, keeping her voice professional. "We're all really happy at the center to see how well Amigo's doing—especially because he had to do it largely alone."

"Alone?" Kev pointed to other winged shadows below. "But I see other condors right there."

"He's got the flock, that's true," Camille said. "But his mate left him while he was still recuperating."

Kev glowered. "Wow, what a bitch."

Camille shook her head. "No, it's not like that. The animal kingdom's a different world. Condors are so rare, it's important for them to find a mate who represents a good investment of their time. Unfortunately, Amigo's mate decided an injured partner was just too much to deal with."

I glanced nervously at Jax. Someone leaving their partner because an injury was too much—it was the kind of fear I worried he might have after the run in with Darrel, and I found myself hoping he wasn't listening, even though the story was just about birds. Fortunately, he still seemed too involved in his games to notice.

"After that," Camille continued, "Amigo's been a fine bird, but not really the same. We've been hoping for years that he'd find a new mate, but it seems like he only had eyes for her."

As I watched, Jax's expression only cracked once—just once, and just for a second, but it was enough. Even as he looked down at his tablet, his fingers swiped faster, agitatedly. Sky gave me an anxious side-eye, mouthing two words in a silent plea: *do something.*

I glanced toward Camille, who seemed totally oblivious to the sudden chill that hung in the air. In a single, fluid motion, I swiped the remote tracker out of her hand. Her mouth opened with surprise, but I gave her a broad grin, hoping she'd mistake my nerves for enthusiasm. "How about that one?" I asked hurriedly. "That bird over there? What's his story?"

One of her eyebrows lifted, but she didn't seem fazed by my sudden interest in condors. "Oh, that one," she said, her eyes flicking down to the readout on the tracker. "You're looking at The Great One. It's funny, we never thought he'd be good at living in the wild."

The Great One swooped down along the shoreline, stopping at a brown form in the distance. He pecked once, then again, at the lump in the sand. "He looks pretty wild to me," Sky said, looking fascinated as she followed the bird's every movement.

Camille chuckled. "Now that he's eating foxes like a condor would in the wild, you'd think so. But you should have seen him when he was a hatchling. He was raised in our center, the first puppet-raised bird to be reintroduced to the wild."

"You mean, like, a *sock* puppet or something?" Chewie asked, his hand in a jaw-like pose to demonstrate.

She looked at his hand appraisingly. "Actually, just like that, except the puppet looked like a mother condor. The Great One was raised in captivity. He never knew his parents."

Sky's eyes softened. "Poor little guy." I looked over toward Jax to see if he was listening, but he'd moved on to a game I'd never seen, with a spaceship racing across the screen, and seemed completely engrossed.

"Not so fast, sis," Chewie spoke up. "Sounds kind of like the easy life to me. Human caretakers to attend to your every need, every meal gourmet."

Camille gave him an odd look. "Well, you know, you're right, life is different in captivity. I wouldn't necessarily say *better*, though." In the distance, The Great One ripped a big piece of flesh from the dead fox. "And it made it much harder to introduce him to the wild."

Jax's low, dark-tinged voice pierced through the sound of the crashing surf. "Maybe he just wasn't ready for it." I felt surprised, and a little relieved, to hear him say anything at all.

Camille gave him a tight-lipped smile. "That's what we thought at first, too," she says. "We worried he wouldn't make it—that he'd assimilate so badly that we'd have to capture him again. Or, worse, that we'd find him dead."

Sky watched as the massive condor arced upward into the sky. "But he looks fine now," she protested.

"He does, doesn't he?" Camille's smile widened. "That's because of The Wild One."

"The Wild One?" Chewie said. "Sounds like my kind of condor."

Camille reached for the remote tracker. "She's probably around here somewhere. Let me take a look."

I handed off the device to her, glad to have it out of my hands—unlike Chewie, I didn't have any particular fondness for gadgets. With it gone, I could stop pretending to care about condors and look back at the man I actually cared about.

To my surprise, Jax's eyes were nowhere near the iPad screen. Instead, I saw him scanning the skies with interest, looking where Camille pointed as she shouted: "There she is! I knew she wouldn't be far from him."

I looked past the cliff's edge until I saw another winged movement below, twisting in a wide circle near the fox corpse. "Ever since The Wild One found The Great One, they've been inseparable," she said. "She was raised by real parents, so she was really the one who could help him understand his heritage, that he was a free bird, not a captive."

In the distance, I heard motorcycles rumbling over the highway, a sound I couldn't hear any more without thinking of the night I'd thrown the Molotov. I glanced back toward Jax, and saw that his dark eyes were piercing right into me. The moment my eyes caught his, though, he averted his gaze downward.

Camille was still talking. "Over there, as you can see—"

"I've had about enough birds." Jax was quiet, but there was force behind his words. "I'm going back to the car."

Concern flooded me. What had made his mood change so suddenly? His face looked like a storm cloud had passed in front of it.

Sky spoke up first. "We'll come with you, Jax. We don't have to stay here. It's just birds."

He shook his head. "Stay. You're having fun. I'll still be waiting when you're finished."

"Are you su—" I started to reach toward Jax's shoulder, but he'd already started walking away. Sky took a deep breath and started talking to Camille like everything was normal. Chewie and Kev quickly followed her lead.

*I wonder if they've had to do this before.* The rest of the band might be able to pretend that nothing had happened, but Jax's unpredictable, erratic behavior had me worried. "Guys, I'm going back to find out what's up with Jax. But you stay here, this place is amazing."

Sky looked at me quickly and gave a short nod. Then I was off.

***

Jax's head was tilted down as I got to the car, and the glow on his face showed me that he was still wrapped up in the gift I'd given him. "Hey," I said as his thumbs twitched rhythmically against the glass. "Can we talk?"

Without changing his rhythm for a moment, Jax spoke. "Sure."

I opened the door and slid into the back seat next to him. "I'd like it better if I could look in your eyes," I said, as gently as I could.

Snarling with frustration, Jax thumb-swiped hard and set the tablet down. "Fine," he said, looking me dead in the face. His hardened look made it clear that he was trying to be tough, but somehow I saw something else there, too: fear and vulnerability. Even though Jax's stoic machismo was his way of dealing with trouble, I couldn't help but see that it had made him anxious and afraid.

"Jax, please just talk to me about what's going on," I said, my voice straining.

He looked away from me. "Look. I know this isn't what you signed up for."

"What's that supposed to mean?"

His eyes were closed, his fingers curling into his palms. "You saw things I never wanted you to see. Now you see me differently."

"I don't see you differently at all. You—"

"You deserve someone who can *protect* you, dammit," he said, looking into my eyes with a haunted gaze. "And instead, you ended up protecting *me*. You can deny it all you want, but I know it has to bother you."

Even though I knew Jax's words came from pain, it still stung to hear that he thought I'd be so heartless. "What are you talking about? That doesn't bother me. I wish I'd done more to get you to the hospital before the show, but that's guilt, not . . . whatever it is you're implying."

"You don't even know the worst of it," Jax said, his voice bitter. "And when you do, you're not going to want to be around me anymore anyway. I'm so fucked up right now."

I looked at him, confused. "What are you talking about?"

"Hell, I'm so fucked up I thought I saw Darrel on the highway for a minute on our way here. I'm fucking nuts, Riley. Can't you see that?" Jax's words sounded desperate, and my heart wrenched with guilt over the way the night with Darrel had gone.

"You're not nuts, Jax," I said, trying to keep my voice even. "You're just having a hard time. Anyone would be, after what you went through."

"Oh yeah?" A tight, bitter laugh escaped Jax's lips, and he stared back down at the dark iPad screen. "Then why are you pulling away from me?"

I put my hand over his. Jax seemed really scared—something I'd done had made him genuinely afraid he'd lose me. Gently, I squeezed his hand. "Why do you think I've been pulling away from you?" I asked softly.

He pulled his hand away. "You keep using this tone with me, like I'm a wounded animal or something. Your voice is soft where it used to be edgy, Pepper. You used to give me sass instead of spending your days worrying about whether I was okay."

"But I *care* about you." My eyes were filling with tears, but I couldn't let them fall. Jax was probably right, I had been treating him with kid gloves. But what was I supposed to do when I didn't want him to get hurt any more than he already had been?

"I know you care." His voice was gruff. "But this isn't just going to be all better. Not today, not tomorrow. Do you understand that? And you can't make me better any faster. I know it's not fun for you. If you want out, just say so."

I took both his hands into both of mine. "I can't make it better. But I can be here for you. I don't understand everything you're going through, but I'm not going anywhere."

His hands tensed. "I don't want to be treated like I'm broken."

"I don't think—" I started speaking gently, but then cut myself off. Was that really what Jax wanted? Jax saw kindness as pity. There had to be some other way to get through to him. An idea occurred to me.

I took my hands out of his. "I don't think you're broken at all." Slowly, I slid my open hand along his thigh, harder than just a gentle caress. I caught Jax's eye and held it as my hand slid up, up, slowly, until I heard his breath go in sharply. "Remember the night we first met?" I whispered.

Jax's eyes, dulled before, flickered to life for an instant. "What are you doing?" he asked with an incredulous look.

"What do you think I'm doing?" I slid my hand up against his fast-rising bulge. "I'm getting you hard."

Jax looked around the parking lot nervously. "Not right now, Riley. I—this may not be a good idea out here."

I leaned forward to the front console of the convertible and pressed a button. "Does this make it better?" I asked, moving to the back seat as the roof started sliding over the car, enclosing us in a bubble of privacy.

"I'm just not sure this will work," he muttered, embarrassed. "Since everything happened, I haven't . . . I mean, we haven't . . . I mean . . ."

I put a finger to my lips. "Shh. You don't have to do anything. I started something the day we met, and today I'm going to finish it."

He looked at me closely, his face a question: *are you sure?*

"Trust me. Just lay back," I said, my face turning into a grin. "You're in good hands."

When I saw him smile back, I pulled his zipper down.

His cock was as magnificent as the first time I'd seen it. *I can't believe I fit that entire thing inside me,* I thought, but the sudden tingling feeling between my legs told me that after so long without his touch, my cravings were as immense as he was.

I licked my hands to make them slippery, then slid them over the head of his cock, making him gasp with pleasure. Slowly, I moved one hand down over the other, keeping them both stroking in a steady rhythm.

"God, I missed feeling you," Jax moaned.

"I missed feeling *you*," I purred against his ear, grasping his cock harder.

As my fingers squeezed over him, Jax's eyes closed tight with pleasure.

Taking my palms away, I traced a line down the underside of his cock with my finger. "Open your eyes, Jax," I said, suddenly realizing exactly how I needed to get through to him.

"What?"

"Open them. Just keep them open."

His eyelids lifted, and dark-rimmed pupils stared into mine. I moved my fingers in tightening waves around the shaft of his cock, and his muscles grew taut, straining against his clothing, as I watched his face—the face of the rock star I'd made mine.

As I moved my thumb and forefinger to the head of his cock, still stroking with my other hand, his gasps grew quicker. Beads of sweat erupted on his forehead, and his breaths were almost a cry.

"Riley, be careful," he said, his words interrupted by shallow breaths. "It's been a long time. You're going to make me come."

"I know," I said. "I want to."

"Band will be back," he panted, his face etched with lines of effort. "Nothing to clean it up with."

"I can think of something," I said, and bent my head down toward his cock. *I want you, Jax. Now do you understand?*

"Oh, God, Riley... I'm not going to last..."

*Good.* If I could get Jax back, the old Jax, the Jax I knew. I kept my hand squeezing firmly as my lips slid around him and I took him into my mouth. His hands fisted into my hair as my tongue skimmed the head, and as I heard him cry out, I brought my lips around him even deeper.

Jax's body jerked, and my mouth filled with the taste of the sea as his fists tightened suddenly, then relaxed.

I swallowed and took my mouth and hands away slowly, straightening in the back seat. Jax looked at me with a mixture of contentment and awe. More importantly, he looked like himself.

"See?" I said, smiling and feeling just a little bit like a world-class sex goddess. "No cleanup needed."

He reached out an arm to put around me, and I nestled in against his body. It took everything I had not to press closer, but I knew that the flesh beneath Jax's shirt was raw and bruised.

It felt like we laid there a long time like that, not saying anything, not moving—just enjoying the feel of our bodies lying next to each other.

After minutes of silence passed, Jax took a deep breath. "I've been thinking about what you said before," he said, giving my shoulder a squeeze.

"Huh?" I said, blinking myself back out of the dreamy reverie I was in.

"About beefing up security for the concert," he said evenly. "I think you may be right."

"Wait, really?"

"It wouldn't hurt. I'll call about it tomorrow."

I narrowed my eyes, wondering what had brought on the sudden change of heart. *Does it really matter? Don't look a gift horse in the mouth.*

"Thank you," I said finally. "That means a lot to me."

Maybe he'd changed his mind because of the sex—but so what if he had? He was right. I'd been treating him like he was made of porcelain ever since the night of the Molotov, and that couldn't feel good.

But at least I'd managed to coax him out of his shell, and for now, even something that small felt like a victory. There was no way for me to know how long it would last, but I did know one thing—I would keep doing whatever it took to make him well again.

# Chapter Eight

## CHANGE

After our stop at Big Sur, we made record time to San Francisco with Chewie happily coaxing as much speed out of the convertible as he could on the winding coastal road.

And for the first time since Jax had brought me to the scene of his darkest secrets, I was happy, too—and it wasn't because of the awesome scenery. The whole rest of the way, Jax held my hand, even when he teased me. He laughed and joked with the band. From the surprised looks everyone shot one another, I could tell that no one was sure what had happened with Jax—not that it stopped us from enjoying it, just the same.

But every time I glanced at Jax's smiling face, I reminded myself of what he'd told me. He still had a long way to go to heal. I shouldn't expect changes overnight. And though the handjob had brought us closer than we'd been all week, we were still far from being back to normal. Not that we'd ever really had a normal relationship, but before all this drama we'd at least been free to simply enjoy each other, without Jax's demons coming between us.

Despite my wariness over Jax's good mood, he continued to surprise me. It stayed with him all through our first night in San Francisco, and even into the next day. And at the radio station where the band had their interview, he surprised me even more.

While answering questions from the pretty female DJ, he positively smouldered, making eyes at me that even made the show host take notice—because she thought it was all for her. As I watched from a seat in the back of the studio, I thought she would melt under the full force of his scorching persona.

*Where did that come from?* Maybe it was the handjob, maybe it was because this was a work situation, after all, but it seemed like my sexy boyfriend was back.

*Don't get too excited.* Jax still had a lot of trauma that he needed to deal with. But it *did* seem like he was improving—he'd even asked me to go out on a date after the interview wrapped up. I knew that Jax could put together one hell of a good evening, so I'd been looking forward to it for most of the day.

When the interview finished, Jax came over to where I sat in the back of the studio.

"Ready to hit the road?" he asked with a smile.

"I'm ready," I said, picking up my purse and standing up. "But I'm still dying to know why you insisted on me wearing sneakers today, instead of sandals. I'm a New Yorker, I can go miles in a pair of espadrilles."

Jax smiled again, a sly one this time. "You'll see. Besides, I think those are cute. They look like clown shoes."

Grimacing, I looked down at my multi-colored feet. The running shoes I'd packed on the off chance that I could squeeze in some exercise on this tour were so brightly neon that they could blind an unwary onlooker. In retrospect, that's probably why they'd been such a bargain—they were hard to look at without getting nauseous.

I raised an eyebrow. "Hopefully wherever we're going doesn't have a dress code."

"If it did, you'd definitely start a new trend," Jax said with a smirk. "Come on, let's go."

He wouldn't say another word about where we were going during the cab ride, but since he had me wear these shoes, I felt fairly certain that wherever we went, we'd be doing a lot of walking.

And when the cab dropped us off, I saw that I wasn't wrong.

I gave a slow whistle. "Wow. We're going all the way up *there*?

We stood at the foot of the steepest hill I'd ever seen. A hill so steep, that the street just stopped, as if the city builders had given up. In its place, a set of wooden stairs snaked their way up to the top. I could just see through the trees a white tower that perched at the hill's summit. He was right, sandals would have been murder on a climb like that.

"Telegraph Hill," Jax said with satisfaction. "And we're going to the top. It's got the best view of the city."

I gave him a sidelong look. "Did the doctor say when you would be ready for something like this?" I looked up again at the dizzying staircase. "There must be like five hundred steps."

"He said it was okay to get some exercise," Jax said. "And this won't be a problem for me." He gave me a smirk that was filled with his usual teasing sense of humor. "Maybe you're the one not up for the challenge."

"I'm not that out of condition yet," I retorted. "I bet I'll still be ready for more when you're wheezing that you can't go on."

Jax's eyes narrowed. "And I bet that you'll be begging me to carry you the last few yards."

I shook my head, smiling. "Not a chance. Care to make it interesting? The one who's hurting the most at the end buys dinner."

"You're on."

On the first flight of stairs, my thigh muscles stretched in a way they hadn't since . . . well, since I'd ridden Jax to orgasmic oblivion in Las Vegas. I smiled with pleasure. Whatever our relationship ended up being like once Jax healed, I wanted that kind of fun to happen often. Daily, even.

My distracting thoughts melted away after about forty steps, when my breath started to hitch. *No, not already!*

"Having problems?" Jax asked, a gleam in his eye. "Need a rest?"

"No," I huffed. "Just getting into the swing of it. Maybe you just want an excuse to stop."

"I'm fine," Jax replied, his voice hardly winded. "This feels great."

I glanced at him. His chest rose and fell easily, and he climbed with an energy usually reserved for his rock shows. Sweat beaded on his forehead, and he took off the button up shirt he wore over his wifebeater without even breaking his stride.

*Damn it, he's been in the hospital and he's in better condition than me.* I grinned to myself, taking in the way his biceps stretched taut under his tan skin. *Not that I'm complaining.*

My breath hitched again, and I concentrated on climbing. Up ahead, a long landing interrupted the flight of stairs, stretching around either side of the hill. Houses jutted out alongside it, making the landing look like a little sidewalk. Maybe I could find a way to rest up there that wouldn't undo our bet.

"Come on," I said, scrambling ahead of Jax, my chest heaving. "I call a truce if there's a good view from up there. We don't want to miss it, right?"

Suddenly, a stinging slap landed on my ass. A cry escaped my lips, and I turned to see Jax grinning at me.

"I like the view just fine from here," he said, his eyes gleaming in a way that I loved to see. This date seemed to be keeping his spirits up . . . if not something else, I thought with a wicked grin.

I rubbed the spot where his hand had landed and arched an eyebrow at him. "So you did have an ulterior motive for coming up here."

"No, that's just one of the perks. I can't help it if you're sticking your butt in my face, asking for it."

I started climbing again, swinging my rear in an exaggerated sway. "If I'm asking for it, then come and get it," I said over my shoulder.

Jax pressed his lips together with determination and made a lunge for me. His hand brushed the back of my leg, but missed as I dodged away from him. Laughing, I turned and ran up the stairs. The sound of Jax's shoes scraping on the wooden stairs as he chased me sent a thrill of excitement through me, and with a sudden burst of energy, I scrambled up onto the landing.

I turned to get my bearings and stopped still. I gazed around in wonder.

A hand reached around my waist, and I jumped. Jax pressed himself against me, his breath hot in my ear.

"Got you," he said, kissing the back of my neck.

I laughed and pointed to the view. "Come on, I call truce. Look."

Jax let go of me with a reluctant sigh, then followed my gaze. A smile lit up his face.

San Francisco Bay stretched before us in a late afternoon glow. Sailboats dotted the water. Trees and bushes obscured the view somewhat, but it was still breathtaking.

I shaded my eyes. "Is that Alcatraz?" I asked, pointing at a distant island.

Jax looked for a moment, then nodded.

I eyed the distance from the island to shore. "I guess it worked as a prison for a reason. No one could escape from there, could they?"

He shrugged. "That's what the officials say."

Tilting my head, I looked up at him. "Is it up for debate?"

Leaning against the railing, Jax stared out at the island. "Rumor has it three men escaped in the sixties." He whipped his head around, giving me an amused look. "Haven't you ever seen *Escape From Alcatraz*? Clint Eastwood?"

I folded my arms across my chest. Old movies weren't really my forte—until I'd met Jax, that is. "No, Mr. Movie Buff, I haven't. But let me guess what it was about. An escape."

Dismissing my sarcasm with a quick smile, Jax nodded. "It's based on real events. These guys dug through the walls, left behind paper mache dummies to fool the guards, and took off across the bay on a raft made out of raincoats."

I gazed back over the wide expanse of water that separated the island from the mainland, and shivered. That looked like a far way to go on just some raincoats stitched together. "No wonder they made a movie about it. And they survived?"

A slow grin appeared on Jax's face. "No one found their bodies, but three men were spotted in a boat on the water that night, then later stealing a truck."

"Maybe they did escape then," I murmured. "It's weird though, those guys were criminals who probably deserved to be locked up, but somehow you just have to root for them anyway. Even if it feels wrong."

"It's the underdog principle," Jax said, drawing his brows together. "The more impossible the odds, the more you want to beat them. And if anyone else tries, you root for them too."

"Even if they've done bad things?"

He nodded, seeming sure of himself. "Everyone deserves a second chance."

I stayed quiet, looking at the island. *Even your dad?* He was the one who'd almost broken Jax. But not quite. Jax was a fighter—he'd survived, despite the odds.

Jax interrupted my thoughts. "So, you're my favorite lockpicker. Think could you break out?"

I laughed, glad for a reason to forget my dark thoughts. "Hah. I can pick a lock, but this place was built for people who knew more than me about escape plans. If I were stuck in there, I'd probably just rot."

He put his arm around my shoulders and kissed the top of my head. "If you couldn't get out, I'd break you out."

"It's reassuring to know my boyfriend will help me plan a jailbreak," I said with a wry smile. Reaching for Jax's waist, I pulled him closer. "Maybe—"

A sharp wolf whistle carried through the air aimed at us, and I stopped, surprised. *Who did that?*

I looked around. We were alone on the landing, and no one climbed the stairs behind us. Jax stared at the steps leading upwards, frowning, but the people walking up them had their backs to us, and were too far away besides.

Jax turned back to me, his brows drawn with annoyance. "That's not —"

The whistle came again, but this time it was louder. And from the direction of one of the small houses that clung to the hillside.

Jax followed my gaze and scowled. "What, is it some asshole peeping Tom?"

The whistle sounded again, but this time my eyes connected it to a flutter of movement in a tree next to the house.

Seated on a branch above our heads was a green bird with a tan curved beak and a blotch of red covering its head.

"A parrot?" I cried.

It squawked in reply, then made another human sounding whistle.

I clutched Jax's arm. "Do you see that? What's it doing out here?"

Jax narrowed his eyes at it. "Someone's taught it to be rude. Shouldn't be whistling at my girl like that."

"Do you think it's lost?" I asked, moving closer to the tree to get a better look at the bird. It cocked its head calmly and regarded me with intelligent eyes. Did it belong to the owner of the house?

"It's too laid back to be lost," Jax observed, a look of understanding dawning over his face.

I shook my head, not buying his take on the situation. "If it's a pet then we should rescue it and bring it to its owner. Maybe the bird doesn't *feel* lost, but he might be just the same."

I gauged where the bird sat perched on a branch above my head. He didn't look *too* high up—maybe I could climb up and get him? Or maybe he'd just come to me. "Here birdie," I coaxed, holding out my hand.

Another squawk sounded on my left, and I whipped my head around. On a branch higher up, another parrot was perched.

I shook my head, amazed at what I saw. One was someone's pet gone missing. Two—did that mean they got loose from a pet shop?

I was startled by the sound of Jax's laughter.

"What's so funny?" I demanded.

"You." He held his side as he laughed.

"I don't know what's funny about helping lost pets."

Jax stopped laughing and wiped his forehead. "So you really haven't heard of these parrots before? It took me a minute, but I figured it out."

I folded my arms impatiently. "I don't know, was it in the paper that someone lost their bird?"

He exhaled and looked at me with amusement. "You've really got to start watching more Netflix. There was a documentary I watched last year on these wild parrots. San

Francisco's got a flock of them that were probably released by their owners, since they were caught wild in South America and didn't turn out to be good pets."

My mouth fell open. I couldn't stand selfish people who bought pets and then dumped them to starve or freeze to death, just because having an animal took too much effort.

"That's awful," I cried, "How could anyone do that?"

Jax shrugged. "These are wild birds, Riley, not puppies. They're actually doing better out here."

I looked up at the parrot perched above my head. It cheerfully began cleaning the feathers on its chest. Okay, it did look pretty content. My outrage faded and was replaced with awe.

"So they're a tough bunch then," I said.

"They know how to survive," he replied dryly, and I glanced up at him, surprised at how he'd unintentionally echoed my earlier thoughts.

"Come on," he continued with a grin, "Let's go. I've still got to win my bet."

As we started up the next flight of stairs, I took one more glance at the parrots. Wild exotic birds weren't exactly what I expected to see out here, but along with Jax's surprising turnaround, so far nothing about this day had turned out the way I thought it would.

The sun began to fade as we climbed. The short rest on the landing had done me good, and I gleefully matched Jax's pace. *We'll see who's going to carry who up the last few flights.*

But keeping up with him had a price. My thighs burned and I had a stitch in my side when I reached the last flight. *One more. Thank fuck.*

With Jax in the lead, I climbed the last few steps, my face flushed and sweat making my shirt stick to my back. At this rate, maybe I'd skip dinner if I won, and just go for a shower.

Then I reached the top. I'd thought climbing the stairs was enough to take my breath away. But that was nothing compared to how I felt when I turned back to look at the new view.

Higher than we were before, now the entire city stretched before us. The Golden Gate Bridge loomed in the distance, silhouetted in the setting sun. Bright reds and yellows tinted the sky, and the sunset colors reflected off the water of the bay.

"It's beautiful," I gasped, holding my aching side.

"It's worth the hike, isn't it?" Jax replied, smiling as he gazed into the distance.

I nodded, unable to find any other words for it. My body tingled, both from the exercise and a sense of awe. The scene had so much natural beauty, but the city sprawling far below somehow made it even more breathtaking.

"You know what this reminds me of?" I asked.

"What?"

"The first time I saw Manhattan from the top of the Empire State Building when I was a kid. I remember feeling so . . . in *love* with New York the minute I saw it. From then on I always knew I wanted to live in the city."

I gazed at the view, sensing Jax as he came up beside me. I spun around and took his hand. "Hey, you know what we should check out? There's a park I like to watch the sunset from in Manhattan. South Cove. It's actually really peaceful."

I laughed. "It's flat though, not much of a hike. I can leave the clown shoes at home."

An emotion I couldn't read flashed across his face, then he smiled and pointed to something out over the bay. "See that down there? That's Fisherman's Wharf."

My face flushed at how neatly he avoided the real subject—one that I hadn't meant to bring up. *He doesn't want to talk about New York.* And why would he? With all his recent worries, making plans about our future had to be the last thing on his mind.

As far as our relationship was concerned, we were still taking it one day at a time. Getting ahead of myself like that—that was something I should avoid if I wanted to keep my peace of mind. Wasn't this date enough? It was a chance for us to act in a way that I hadn't been sure we could—like a normal couple.

Jax squeezed my hand, interrupting my reverie. "Hey, you forgot something."

I glanced up at him, hoping that he would think my flushed face came from our climb. "What?"

A grin lit up his face. "You owe me dinner."

My eyes widened. *That sneak.* I let go of his hand and took a step back. "Wait a minute, where do you get that?" I pointed to the wifebeater that clung to his chest. "You're sweating buckets just like I am."

"Yeah, but I wasn't wheezing as much as you either. I thought you'd need a respirator by the time we got up here."

I smiled. "And who was that huffing and puffing behind me?" I held out my hand. "I call it a draw. Let's go dutch."

Jax laughed and shook my hand. "Maybe you should have gone into law instead of accounting."

I stepped closer, and he put a hand on my waist, pulling me towards him. His lips settled onto mine, softly probing, and a warmth rippled through my body. I brought my hand up, tugging at his hair, and his kiss became more fierce. Almost possessive, like he couldn't get enough of me.

*I can't get enough of him either. Ever.*

As he kissed me, suddenly it didn't matter that we weren't talking about the future yet. We had this day.

And it was perfect.

# Chapter Nine

### NIGHTFALL

After our visit to Telegraph Hill, Jax and I grabbed bacon-wrapped hot dogs from a street vendor for dinner before we met up with the band again—and even though he tried to back out on our deal and pay for the whole thing himself, I stuck to my guns. We went dutch.

Even though I would have loved to stay in San Francisco another night, we had to hit the road, despite the late hour. Reed wanted us back in LA for another promo at one o'clock tomorrow, and Kev volunteered to drive us through the night so that we could get some extra sleep on the bus before that happened.

It was 2:30 when we pulled up to our new digs—Reed's house in Malibu. Bernie had parked the bus there in the driveway for us, and we all stumbled onto it and up to bed, exhausted. Before I fell asleep, I wondered what the inside of Reed's house looked like—if it would be at all as flashy as the man.

Then I drifted off, happy to be back in the Fortress of Solitude, snuggling up next to Jax in our bed.

*Thud!*

My eyes shot open. The room was dark.

A groan came from my left. *What was that?*

*Whack!*

I rolled over, fumbling for the lamp a moment before I could switch it on.

Jax stood by the closet. His eyes were closed, and he swayed on his feet.

"Jax, what are you doing up?" I asked groggily.

He didn't answer me, or even move his head like he'd heard me. I blinked and peered at him. His face was pale, and his eyes were screwed shut.

A creepy sensation filled my stomach. Was he even awake?

"Baby," I said, my voice quavering a little. "What's going on?"

His swaying increased, and he shook his head back and forth violently. "No," he said in a strange, high voice. "No, stop."

The hair on the back of my arms pricked up and I shuddered. He sounded so eerie.

I sat up in bed, staring at him as he swayed back and forth like he was in a trance. Was this what sleepwalking looked like?

"Stop!" Jax cried, again in that weird voice, then threw a lightning fast fist at the wall that connected with a dull thud.

My eyes widened with shock. His stayed firmly closed.

This was no regular bad dream—it was a full-on, panic-inducing nightmare. And it was gripping Jax hard. He was hurting himself and he didn't even know it.

A low, keening noise emerged from Jax's throat. Head down, he pressed his scraped, swollen fingers against the wall, the corded veins in his arms popping with the strain.

My heart thudded in my chest. I had to wake him up right away. What if he broke his hand, punching the wall?

Cautiously I crept down to the edge of the bed until I was behind Jax and to his left. I leaned forward and reached out my hand tentatively, hoping to dart in and give him a nudge in his side.

But Jax staggered back, swinging his arms like he was fighting off an invisible assailant. One fist swung in a jagged arc, coming close to my head.

I ducked. His fast moving fist sent a rush of air just inches past my face.

*Holy shit!*

I froze as Jax regained his balance and threw himself back at the wall. His body twisted in torment, and his shoulders hunched as if he was trying to hide from unseen blows.

His eerie, childlike voice filled the room again. "Daddy," he panted, "I'll be good, I promise, just stop hurting me."

His pleading tore at my heart. I moved to reach for him but stopped, my pulse racing. If I got closer, he might hit me by accident. "Jax, wake up!" I shouted.

"No, stop!" Jax moaned, completely oblivious. With a violent and sickening thrust he banged his head into the wall.

I flung myself to my feet and wrenched his shoulders, pulling him back.

Groaning, he tore himself away from me, but then tripped and collapsed in a heap of heaving limbs on the floor.

"Please don't," he moaned, his voice still coming from the depths of his nightmare.

My heart felt like it was going to break in two as I kneeled down on the floor beside him. Jax was being tormented by his old, implacable enemy: his dad. *That bastard.*

I gripped his shoulders and shook him so that his head rolled from side to side. "Wake up!" I cried. His eyes stayed closed. I placed my hand on the back of his neck and stroked his sweat soaked skin. "C'mon, wake up," I pleaded into his ear.

All of a sudden his eyes snapped open. They were wild and staring. His chest heaved up and down, but he was awake.

"Just breathe, baby," I murmured with relief as I ran my hand through his tangled hair. My fingers searched for any cuts, but he was fine, thank god.

Jax closed his eyes again for a moment. When he opened them again, the scary distant look had faded.

He stared at me. "What . . . why am I down here?"

I caressed his cheek softly with a trembling hand. "You were having a nightmare. You got up, started hitting the wall. You were hurting yourself."

Jax's jaw clenched and his nostrils flared as he looked at me with wide, anguished eyes. I winced at seeing so much hurt in them, but then I shook myself. He needed me to be strong.

"C'mon, let's get you up." I took a wide stance and grabbed his hands, bracing myself to haul him to his feet. When he was standing, I gently pushed on his shoulders so that he sat on the edge of the bed.

Tremors ran through his body. Jax held up a shaking hand and stared at his scraped knuckles. His eyes widened, and his face blanched. "Did I hurt you?" he cried.

His desperate expression made me quickly drop down next to him on the bed. I rubbed his thigh. "No baby, it's alright. I'm fine."

Jax hunched over and rested his head in his hands. His squeezed his eyes shut tight. "Thank god," he whispered.

I shivered a little, remembering my close call with his fist, and draped my arm around his shoulders. It all felt so unreal. I'd thought he was getting better, but now I knew how wrong I was. It wasn't enough that Darrel had hurt Jax day in and day out in waking life, now he was possessing Jax's dreams. Making him lash out in pain. I closed my eyes as a shudder jerked through my body. I couldn't imagine how deep that pain must go.

A soft knock on the door made me jump.

I took a deep breath and squeezed Jax's shoulder. He didn't look up as I stood and opened the door a crack.

Kev was standing there in his boxer shorts. One piece of his blonde hair stuck straight up. His eyes were sleepy.

"What was that noise?" he asked in a drowsy voice.

I gripped the door knob tightly to control my trembling fingers and opened the door a little wider, but not enough for Kev to see into the room. I knew Jax would want privacy.

I forced my voice to sound calm. "Jax had a nightmare, but it's okay now."

His eyes flickered with concern. "It sounded pretty bad."

"I know," I replied with a weak shrug. "He gets them sometimes. Sorry it was loud."

"Oh, no worries. I just wanted to see if everything was okay." Kev's eyes grew heavy again.

If I kept him standing here, he'd pass out on his feet. "Thanks, I appreciate it. Goodnight."

"Mmhmm. Night."

Kev turned to go, and I sighed as I shut our door, relieved that Jax and I were alone again.

He still sat with his head in his hands, but now his broad fingers were pressed hard against his closed eyes. It looked like he wanted to escape from the terrible visions that were forcing themselves on him. The sound of his shallow and strenuous breathing filled the room, as if he found the close air to be suffocating.

I sat down next to him, and rubbed his back. "Hey," I said softly. "C'mon, let's go to the roof. It's a little stuffy in here, don't you think? Some fresh air would be good."

He picked his head up and looked at me with a haunted expression before nodding. "Yeah, okay."

We quietly headed up to the deck, taking care not to disturb the rest of the band.

Up there the night air was cool, with just a hint of breeze. Jax threw himself down on the edge of a lounge chair, and I dragged another one for myself next to his.

He didn't say a word, but he took in big gulps of the refreshing air. From his unusual pallor and the deep furrows in his brow as he stared at the deck floor, I could tell that the demons from his nightmare were still gripping him tightly.

I kept my gaze trained on Jax, uneasily watching his signs of distress. He sat rigidly in the chair, his hands flexing and clenching on the armrests, his face still unnaturally pale.

He was trying to keep his composure in front of me, but I could tell he was hanging on by a thread. I wanted to help him, but I didn't know what to do. I felt helpless. And whatever helplessness I was feeling, I knew Jax was feeling a hundred times worse.

As the moments stretched out in silence, I could see by Jax's tense posture that the deep breathing wasn't helping him calm down.

I reached out and covered his hand with mine. He jumped, and looked at me with startled eyes.

"Sorry," I murmured, drawing my hand away.

He exhaled slowly. "Don't worry about it."

I settled back in my chair, my brow furrowed. It hurt to see him so tense and miserable. There *had* to be something I could do to help.

My eyes roamed around the deck, looking for a way to distract him from his pain. I squinted at the bar behind him. Bernie kept it stocked with every kind of liquor Jax liked.

Then my eyes fell on a ceramic ashtray resting on top of the bar. Inside was resting a half-smoked joint.

Perfect. This could be just the medicine he needed.

I scooped it up and held it out to Jax like I had found a prize. "Look," I said as I snapped up a lighter that was next to the ashtray. A few quick puffs and the joint was lit.

I leaned back in my chair and took a big drag. "Damn," I said, coughing as I exhaled. I was still a relative newbie when it came to smoking pot. "Chewie outdid himself. Want to try?"

I held out the joint to Jax. He stared at the glowing tip for a second, then reached out and plucked it from between my fingers.

He took a deep, long drag, and a cloud of smoke curled around his head as he exhaled. His eyes squeezed shut briefly, and he nodded a thanks before offering it back to me with shaking hands.

Our fingers brushed, and the image of us sharing a smoke like this outside of Denver flashed before my eyes. The connection between us had been so simple back then. Just a guy getting to know a girl. And now we were locked in a battle against Jax's past.

I took another quick puff on the joint before passing it back to Jax.

He sighed deeply and took one more slow hit. His back was hunched as he sat on the edge of the lounge chair, and suddenly I had another idea.

I stood up and moved over to Jax, softly placing my hands on his shoulders as I lowered myself behind him. From this position I began kneading his neck with firm movements.

He groaned a little and hung his head forward as I worked him over. Other than that, he stayed quiet, and I cast about for an amusing story to distract him with.

"Hey," I said in as upbeat a voice as I could manage, "did the guys ever ask you to settle their debate?"

Jax opened his mouth slightly, then paused and licked his lips. "No," he said in a thick voice.

I moved my hands in small circles, easing the knots as I found them. His body slowly started to relax under my touch.

"Hmm, well, you might want to get in on this. You are the band leader, after all."

He took another long drag on the joint, holding it loosely between his fingers. "What debate?"

"The guys went to a strip club a few days ago and saw a show."

I adjusted my rhythm and increased the pressure of my movements on his back. He groaned a little in relief as I touched a sensitive spot, then nodded his head, indicating that I should go on.

That encouraged me, so I continued with more enthusiasm. "It must have been good, because Chewie came back with the brilliant idea to hire a couple of girls as background dancers for the Hitchcocks."

A shadow of a smile hinted around his lips as he turned his head briefly. His muscles relaxed a little more under my fingers as I pressed into the small of his back.

"So what do you think, would that amp up the show?" I asked.

"I like the show the way it is," Jax said with a slight shrug.

I moved my hands back up to his shoulders, glad to find that most of his tension there had evaporated. I lifted a hand to gently brush his tangled hair behind his left ear. "Then you'd better tell that to Chewie. He's got Kev half convinced that Amber and Coco would be a great addition."

Jax sighed. "Maybe next tour."

He was quiet after that, and I didn't know what else to say. I guess it hadn't been enough to get his mind off his problems. I focused instead on really digging in and kneading his neck. *Well, at least I can do this.*

Then Jax shifted under my hands. "But I guess I wouldn't mind doing a few interviews," he said in a quiet voice.

I stared at the back of his head. Was that a joke?

From the trace of a smile that haunted his lips as he turned to me, I had to say yes. I swallowed, then gave a throaty laugh. "You still have a fondness for lining up women."

He shrugged, and I moved my hands to his shoulders. "They can try out solo."

"Well, I'm sure the guys won't mind that."

This time the conversation really was over because Jax didn't follow up on my comment. But his body under my hands had relaxed, and I felt confident I'd dragged him away from his troubles, at least for a bit.

Jax turned slightly as he took another puff on the joint, and the shadows played across his face, hiding the new marks he'd made on his forehead.

But even if they were hidden, I knew they were there. The image of Jax in torment, banging his head on the wall, leaped back into my mind. There was nothing stopping Jax from hurting himself again if he was caught in the throes of a nightmare.

I frowned in concentration as I continued my kneading. After our San Francisco trip, I'd thought that I'd really been helping him, but maybe I could only provide temporary relief. I had to face the problem squarely—it wouldn't go away with a couple of puffs and an amateur massage. The truth was, even if I had been named the best girlfriend in the world, I wouldn't be able to fight his demons for him. So how would Jax get through this?

My fingers involuntarily tightened on his shoulders as an idea occurred to me. Deep problems like his were never fixed with an instant cure. They required time, and lots of hard, personal work before any progress could be made.

I sucked in a breath. When I began to speak I forced myself to sound casual. "You know, I always wonder how you do it."

"Do what?"

"You're a cocky son of a bitch," I said with a teasing laugh, "But you're also thoughtful, romantic. That's what I like about you, how you can mix it up like that. I never want you to change because I like the whole package."

"That's good."

I paused a moment. "When I was going through my stuff over Connor, it was really hard to accept the good and the bad stuff about myself. I thought it was *all* bad, unfortunately, and I was having a hard time because of it. I tried to get over it on my own, but I couldn't. I needed help."

He didn't respond, but shifted under my hands. I could feel his muscles tense up a bit.

I chose my next words carefully as I kept my fingers working, dropping down to his lower back. "That's why I went to therapy. I was confused and I needed to hear a new perspective." I swallowed. "It helped me so much. I think it might help you too."

While I was talking my hand had paused to rest on his waist. Jax placed his hand over mine, pressing it to his body. He gave it a tight squeeze. The touch wasn't a yes, or a no, but I knew at least he'd been listening.

I released the breath I'd been holding and squeezed him back.

Jax leaned forward and stubbed out the remains of the joint on the deck floor. Then he sighed, and leaned back, stretching out on the lounge chair next to me. He closed his eyes.

I curled up next to him, and he rolled over onto his side, facing away from me. I put my hand on his thigh and drew him into the curve of my hips, enjoying the smooth warmth we created together.

He sighed again as I cradled his body against mine. I could feel his shallow breathing, but his body was relaxed, and after a few moments he had fallen into an exhausted sleep.

I pressed my cheek into his shoulder, grateful he was getting a momentary respite from his pain. But I knew we had a long road ahead of us. His demons had crept into the Fortress of Solitude during the night, attacking Jax at his most vulnerable. Even though they were gone for now, I knew they'd come back.

Staring up at the sky, I resigned myself to gaze at the unfamiliar stars that dotted the darkness above. Sleep for me would be a long time coming.

# Chapter Ten

## STORM

When I woke up, stiff and sore from being camped out on the deck chair, Jax was gone.

Confused, I rubbed my eyes and blinked. In the morning daylight, I could see a glimpse of ocean surf through the palm trees that lined Reed's driveway. *So this is Malibu.*

But I didn't really care about scenery at the moment. What I wanted was to find Jax, and see how he was doing after last night's ordeal. At least I knew he'd gotten a little sleep, up on the deck with me, and that must have helped.

Yawning, I got up and stretched before heading down to the Fortress of Solitude, expecting that Jax had woken up earlier than me as usual and had gone back to the room. But when I opened the door, I found he wasn't there either.

"Jax?" I called out, looking out the window for any sign of him as I started down the stairs. As I got to the bottom, I heard murmured voices. Chewie, Sky, and Kev sat on the black leather couches, talking in hushed, low tones.

Sky's eyes were red and puffy as she said something I couldn't hear. "It's not so bad, sis," Chewie said, his voice more soothing than I'd ever heard it before. "He'll be better in a few hours. You know that. He always is."

I knew with a sinking feeling that they were talking about Jax. Sky's voice trembled, but this time it was loud enough for me to hear from my perch on the stairs. "But what if he's *not*? He seems so much worse this time . . ."

From the lowest stair, I decided to make my presence known. "What's going on?" I asked, trying to sound more nonchalant than I felt.

The band looked up at me, and I suddenly wondered if I'd said something wrong. Chewie muttered something under his breath, but the only word I could make out was "guitar."

Kev snorted. "Jax thinks none of the guitars sound right."

*That's weird.* Jax had been a bit of a musical perfectionist, but I'd never heard him complain about his instruments before. "What, like they're tuned wrong or something?"

"Hell if I know," Kev said, a tinge of annoyance creeping into his voice. "They sounded fine to me. But according to him, everything he plays sounds like shit."

My brow furrowed. *That doesn't sound like Jax at all.* "Where is he now?" I asked.

"Still playing, I think," Sky sniffled. "We just couldn't deal with it any more. I tried to talk to him about it, but . . ."

"But you know how big Jax is on talking," Chewie concluded.

"He's just being a drama queen," Kev said, sounding sure of himself. "He needs to pull himself together. What happened to him on stage could have happened to anyone."

"But it *didn't* happen to anyone," Sky said, sounding dismayed. "It happened to Jax. And we need to be here for him! But I don't know how, when he's acting like . . . like . . . " She looked like she was about to burst into tears.

I frowned with concern. Nothing the band was saying made any sense—I needed to figure out what was really going on. "I'm going in there," I said, making up my mind as the words came out.

"I wouldn't if I were you," said Kev.

Chewie nodded. "Yeah, leave it to work it out on his own. Why do girls always gotta make guys talk about everything?"

Sky shot him a glare through red eyes. "I think it's a good idea," she said to me. "Just be careful, okay?"

I nodded and opened the bus door, stepping out into a cool morning breeze. Reed's house was a sprawling glass-and-steel mansion in a super-modern style cantilevered from the cliffside—as spectacular, and as gaudy, as the man himself. Last night, I'd been wanting to see the inside, but now I took slow steps, each more nervous than the last. Was the band right? Was talking to Jax just a waste of time? I'd spent last night talking to him, but it hadn't seemed to help at all.

As I approached the door, a flurry of notes came through. I recognized the tune: it was the first guitar solo from "Glass Brick," one of the biggest crowd-pleasers at Hitchcocks shows. I stood just outside the doorway, closing my eyes and taking in the music with a deep breath of salt air.

If this was really about the instruments sounding bad, he'd clearly found a way to fix the problem. The song was one of my favorites from the band's set list, and Jax's guitar sounded better than I'd ever heard it in concert. I couldn't keep visions of Jax out of my head—the way he looked during a solo, the concentration, the sweat, a sexuality and urgency in his playing that no one else could match. The music built to the climactic solo crescendo, the riff growing louder, faster, rougher, harder . . .

*BAM!* With a huge crash, the flow of notes stopped and exploded into a brief, tuneless twang that made my heart stop.

I flung the door open, terrified that Jax had somehow injured himself again while playing.

What I saw scared me even worse. Jax was nowhere to be seen, but the aftermath of his playing was everywhere: tuning knobs scattered like marbles next to smashed fretboards, curled-up strings streaming limply from splintered wood. My stomach churned. If Jax had started this guitar massacre while the band was still in the house, it was no wonder they'd decided to leave.

Stepping gingerly to avoid the wreckage, I made my way through Reed's massive living room. As I walked past a curved wall covered in a large painting with a huge rip running through it, I spotted Jax standing in the furthest corner of the room, still holding a guitar neck in his hands.

When he saw me, he froze, the anger in his face mingling with a sudden flash of pain. He said nothing, but looked down at the pieces in his hand and threw them dismissively into a corner. His eyes looked haunted, like they had last night.

I swallowed hard. This was clearly about something more than guitars. Something had pushed him over the edge, and now he was destroying Reed's house, upsetting the band, and tormenting himself. Whatever the reason, it had to stop.

I took a deep breath. "Need any help smashing stuff?" I asked, stuffing my hands deep into my pockets as I tried to force my voice into nonchalance. "I've got a pretty good arm."

He closed his eyes and took several deep breaths before responding, and in the tightness of his jaw I could see he was fighting to let go of his anger. When he opened his eyes again, the fury in them had diminished, but the pain still lingered. "It's all such shit," he said with quiet intensity. "I can't fucking stand it today."

"What happened?" I asked, hoping half-heartedly that maybe there was an easy explanation for this carnage after all. "Did the roadies mess the guitars up?"

"No, I messed it up," he said, gritting his teeth. "Every time I play, I sound like shit."

I looked into his eyes, and saw fear suddenly mixing with the pain. Was I wrong about Jax not being broken by his dad? He was a survivor, it was true, but somehow at that moment he looked just as broken as the guitars on the ground. I could tell he needed help. But how could I possibly give him what he needed when I had no idea what it was?

I walked over to one of the unsmashed guitars and ran my hand over the neck before picking it up. "Maybe you just don't remember what sounding like shit sounds like," I said, trying to stay nonchalant as I slung the strap over my shoulder. "Now, me, on the other hand. . ."

I gripped the frets awkwardly and strummed my fingers over the pickups, creating a noise that sounded like squealing tires, only less pleasant.

Jax flinched at the discordant notes, but he didn't say anything.

*Looks like you need a little more convincing.* "Compared to me, your worst day is like Clapton." I started playing air guitar and did my best impression of the guitar riff from "Layla." "Doodle-deedle-doodle-dee, *deee* doo doo doo dooooo . . . see, that's you."

He closed his eyes and swallowed, as if making another effort to get hold of himself. "You're not even holding that right," he said at last.

I raised an eyebrow. "Not all of us can be rock stars."

"Here, just . . ." he stepped toward me and adjusted the position of the guitar neck in my hand, moving my thumb until it was under the neck instead of over it. "If you hold it the way you were, you'll never get a good sound."

"Oh," I said, relieved I'd been able to make Jax think about something else, even for a minute. "So now I just . . ."

I strummed once more . . . and immediately winced. This time, the sound wasn't quite as horrible—but it wasn't exactly music, either.

Jax cringed, clearly unready for how bad it sounded. "Have you really never played a guitar before?"

"Is that really so surprising?"

He shook his head as if the thought had never occurred to him. "I guess I've just been in the industry too long."

I suddenly felt a little embarrassed. It was easy to forget, sometimes, what different worlds Jax and I lived in. If anyone at my office had ever so much as picked up a guitar, it would have been news to me. "I know you're not going to believe me," I said, grimacing, "but I'm not even a hundred percent sure what a chord is. I'm musically hopeless."

For the first time all morning, the barest hint of a smile traced across his face. "Here, I'll show you one," he said, and put his hands on mine again. This time, he moved them more intricately, and the warmth of his fingers as they subtly positioned mine over the frets sent a thrill coursing through me.

"Good," he said, when he was satisfied with my hand's new position. "Now, strum it again."

Preparing for the worst, I ran my hand over the strings again. This time, what came out of the guitar was definitely more harmonious, even if I wouldn't exactly have wanted to listen to it on CD. "Hey, cool," I said, strumming the notes again.

"That's a C chord," Jax said. "Or it would be, but you have to not pluck the last string when you play. Here, take a pick, it'll make things easier."

I tried again, this time skipping the sixth string with the guitar pick. "Wow," I said. "It's actually music." Fascinated, I plucked the strings over and over, pleased that I could make something that sounded okay—even if it was only one chord. Even with the broken guitars surrounding us, I was starting to feel a little bit better.

"Funny how that works," he said with a wry smile. "You're not bad, for a beginner. Want to learn another?"

I laughed in spite of myself. "How many of these are there? I don't even know if I'll remember how to play this one."

"A lot," Jax admitted. Then, smirking, he said: "But you really only need three, maybe four to start a band."

My lower lip curled with skepticism. "Three or four? That doesn't sound right."

"Here," he said, grabbing another unbroken guitar from the wall and strapping it on. "I'll prove it to you."

A music lesson wasn't what I'd planned on, but if it made Jax's eyes light up that way again, it was more than worth it. He positioned his fingers identically to mine. "This is C, like you just played," he said, then moved his hand to a new spot. "But now *this* . . . is D."

I squinted at his callused fingers. How many times, I wondered, had he made these same chords, practiced them into perfection? Ten thousand? Millions? Awkwardly adjusting, I tried to put my hand into the same new pose. "Like this?"

"Almost," he said with a quick nod. "Put your ring finger a little up . . . Yeah, like that. And now this time, only use the first four strings."

This time, when I plucked the strings, Jax did it at the same time. Both our guitars rang out with a bold sound. I grinned. "This is kind of fun."

"Now, here's the tricky one," he said, his eyes sparkling roguishly. "You ready?"

I nodded with a smile. Whatever else might be wrong with Jax, it was clear that his passion for music was as strong as ever—and somehow, that gave me hope. Music had healed him in the past, maybe it could do the same now.

"For this one, you'll want to make sure your fingers only touch the right frets. Here's the G chord," he said, reaching one finger all the way across the neck of the guitar. "See how my finger has to go all the way to the last string? Now you try."

Stretching my finger to the last string made my hand ache, but after a few seconds, I had my hand in a passable imitation of Jax's. I looked down and suddenly became very aware of the way my middle finger looked. "This one looks like I'm flipping you off," I said with a giggle. "How many strings do I play this time?"

"On a G? All of them."

Making sure my hand was locked into position on the frets, I windmilled my other arm around in an exaggerated motion, bringing the pick down hard over the strings. "Yeah!" I shouted, pumping my fist. The sound was far from perfect, but I felt a swelling sense of pride anyhow. I'd started the day not even knowing what a chord was, and now I'd played three.

"There you go," Jax said, smiling crookedly. "Needs a little work, but you've basically got it. So now, we take the C, the D, and the G . . ."

His fingers moved roughly against the frets as he played the chords in turn. After a moment, I recognized a familiar tune and started to laugh. "I know that one! Bruno Mars."

"Yup. The Lazy Song," he said. "And you already know how to play it—well, almost, anyway. It's all just those three chords, so you'll just have to practice switching them up."

I looked down at the guitar, moving my fingers through the patterns he'd taught me, not plucking the strings, just feeling out the ways my hand position changed from chord to chord. As I tried to practice the fingerwork, Jax started strumming again—only this time, what came out of his guitar was unmistakably "Sweet Home Alabama."

"I didn't really picture you as the southern rock type," I said.

"How about the Johnny Cash type?" he asked, switching the tune to "Ring of Fire." "It's all the same chords, just different patterns."

My eyes widened in surprise. "Holy crap," I said. "Those are all the *same* chords we were just doing? All three of those songs?"

"Yeah," he said. "And there's lots more, too. La Bamba . . . Semi-Charmed Life . . . Wild Thing. . ."

With each new title, he played a few bars. I couldn't help but be impressed, even if it was only three chords. "You sound amazing."

A darkness seemed to pass over Jax's face. "I sound . . . " He cut himself off, shaking his head. "Thanks."

Stepping over a shattered guitar neck, I leaned in and gave him a peck on the cheek. "I don't suppose you have any tricks that could make me sound less like a stepped-on cat when I sing," I said sardonically.

He raised his scarred brow. "It can't be *that* bad."

I arched my brow back at him, as if to say, *Wanna bet?* Without another word, I started in on one of the Hitchcocks' songs:

> *How can you lose what you've never had?*
> *Is this where things get strange—*
> *And I'm lost all the same*

My voice wobbled and warbled all over the place—I couldn't carry a tune in a bucket. Jax tried to smile, but there was cringe written all over his face. *Told you*, I thought, then moved to the big crescendo:

> *Like a train off the tracks*
> *I can never go back*
> *And who is really to blame*

As I hit the high note, my voice cracked hard, forcing a sound more like a death rattle than a song. The smile on Jax's face widened, his eyes crinkled, and suddenly his laughter rang out loud. Though he put his hand over his mouth to stifle it, he couldn't help it—the laugh continued, growing deeper, louder, echoing off the stucco walls until he clutched at his sore side. It had sounded *terrible*—even I had to giggle, and soon realized I couldn't stop.

He wrapped me in his arms, still grinning. "You're just what I needed."

I looked up at him, not sure whether he was being serious. "What, someone to sing an off-key song?"

"No," he said quietly, bending to kiss the top of my head. "A second chance."

Warmth radiated through me, and I stayed quiet in his arms, not wanting to break the silence or end the moment.

When Jax spoke again, his voice was low and intimate. "I'm sorry, Riley. I know the way I've acted this week has been hard on you. On the band, too."

"Jax, you don't have to—"

He shook his head. "Yes, I do. This is too much. I know something has to change. And I think you were right."

I had no idea what he was talking about. "Right about what?"

He closed his eyes tightly, as if what he was about to say was causing him physical pain. "I . . . I saw Darrel today. Again."

My heart started beating practically out of my chest. "What? Where?"

"No. You . . . you don't understand. I thought I saw him. I thought I saw his bike, but I don't think anyone else saw him. I think this is just me." Grabbing a hip flask of liquor, he took a swig and stretched his neck. "This isn't something I can handle on my own. So I . . . I'm going to talk to Reed. He can find me a therapist. He's always telling me he knows everyone worth knowing."

I almost gasped. Even if he was seeing things . . . Jax was *okay* with going to therapy? From the way he'd acted last night, I thought it was going to be nearly impossible to get him to agree to talk about his past to a total stranger, no matter how much he needed it. "You know I think it's a good place to start," I said cautiously, looking around Reed's debris-covered living room. "But don't you think Reed's going to be pissed about all . . ." I gestured to the smashed guitars and the torn painting.

"What, this?" Jax said, shrugging. "It looks better than it ever has after a Grammys after-party. He's seen worse. He'll get over it."

I felt a bit stunned. If I'd done anything to damage my boss Palmer's house, I'd have been collecting unemployment the next day, but Jax could destroy his manager's living room without even thinking twice. "I guess it's different for rock stars," I mused aloud.

His eyes closed. "Some of it, yeah," he said, sounding serious. "But not everything. There's something else I need to talk to you about."

Jax's tone worried me. "What's wrong?"

"I never want to hurt you, Riley." He opened his eyes to look at me again. "It's my worst fear."

I squeezed his hand, but didn't say anything.

"I can't control my nightmares," he continued. "Not yet. And I don't want you to be afraid that I could hurt you because of them."

I wanted to tell Jax that I wasn't even a little afraid after what happened earlier, but it wasn't true. I looked down at the ground.

"I'm going to sleep on the deck chairs by the hot tub." His voice sounded like he'd already made up his mind.

I thought of Jax next to me in the bed, how I'd gotten used to the lines of his body as we spooned together . . .

"But I'll miss you," I blurted out, tears blurring my vision.

"It's not forever," Jax said gently, wiping away a tear. "Just for a few days. Just until I can be sure I won't . . ." His fists balled as his eyes closed again, and he looked close to breaking down. After a deep breath, he started again. "I'm going to keep you safe. Even if it's me you need to be safe from."

I wanted to object—to tell him, no, it was fine, I'd risk him being in the bed with me, even if his nightmares got worse—but looking into his eyes, it was clear that he was serious. And seriously terrified. I almost told him I loved him right then and there. Instead, I bit my lip and whispered:

"Thank you, Jax."

Closing my eyes, I pressed in tight against his body, feeling the warmth of his skin, the taut muscles beneath. The house around us was a disaster, a whirlwind—but here, in the center of the room, in our embrace, we had somehow found the eye of the storm together.

# Chapter Eleven

### IN THE DARK

"Are you sure this is going to work?" Jax lowered himself onto the floor of the car, ducking low enough that his head was impossible to see as soon as the doors were closed.

"Trust me," I said, getting in after him and squeezing myself in next to him on the floor mats. "Besides, anything's better than being trapped in Malibu for another night."

I wasn't the only one who was feeling stir-crazy. Ever since the *Weekly Star* had hit the stands with an expose from an anonymous source, claiming Jax's fall had been the result of a spiraling heroin addiction, the bus had stayed parked in Reed's driveway, waiting for the hordes of paparazzi to find a new flavor of the week.

Unfortunately, it looked like they weren't going away anytime soon—and Jax was in no mood to smile for the cameras. He'd already ventured out on two afternoons, heading to the therapist Reed had recommended, and each time he'd come back with a scowl on his face, swearing about "those damn vultures."

I felt bad that he had to deal with that, but he seemed determined to make therapy work, no matter what got in his way. He came back from each session pensive and withdrawn, but it was early yet, and I knew it would take time before he made any real progress.

But that didn't stop me from missing him every night we slept apart. My brain told me that Jax needed this, that he wanted to keep me safe—but my heart told me that the safest place was in the warmth of his embrace.

In spite of my loneliness at night, I was more than grateful for his efforts to heal. It meant so much to me that he was trying, and I wanted to help in any way I could. I knew Jax was feeling stir crazy—so I'd spent the last few days devising a plan to get us some alone time away from the paparazzi's ever constant presence. It took some doing, but I finally hit upon a way that just might work.

As my legs tangled against Jax's on the car floor, Bernie tossed a blanket back to us. "You kids ready?" he asked with a kindly smile.

"Ready as we'll ever be," I said, spreading the blanket over Jax and me on the car floor. "Let's get the hell out of here."

The car's engine roared to life, and Bernie drove slowly out of the driveway and toward the main gate. From beneath the blanket, Jax held my hands in his, the warmth of his breath heating the darkened space.

Voices grew louder as the car slowed for the gate. "Is he in there?" one voice shouted, and another responded: "No, just the driver this time! False alarm!"

*They sound so disappointed*, I thought with a smug glow of satisfaction. Outwitting the paparazzi wasn't a skill I'd ever thought I'd need, but if this tour had taught me anything, it's that there was a first time for everything.

The car revved to life and suddenly we felt the rush of acceleration as Bernie picked up speed. "The coast is clear, you guys," Bernie called back.

Jax and I took the blanket off our heads simultaneously and looked at each other, silly grins on our faces. "See? Told you," I said. "It was almost too easy."

Jax shook his head, still smiling. "Yeah, but you still haven't told me how you'll keep them away when we actually get where we're going. This is Los Angeles. No matter where we go, there's someone with a telephoto lens trying for a shot."

"Mmhmm," I said, my eyes dancing cryptically. "I guess you'll just have to wait and find out what I have planned."

He raised a questioning eyebrow at me, but my lips were sealed as Bernie wound his way along the coast. I'd planned tonight out meticulously, painfully aware that this date was probably the last one we'd be able to make time for on this tour. We had six days until the festival gig, but with the paparazzi lurking around, and the band needing to practice, there was no telling when we'd be able to snag anymore alone time.

I snuggled in tightly against Jax, my mind playing the last few weeks in my head over and over. We'd come so far, and the thousands of miles we'd traveled were just the start. Emotionally, I'd traveled an even longer road. I'd never felt so protected by anyone—or so protective of them. I'd never wanted so badly for a relationship to continue.

But I knew, with every passing mile and minute, that the end of the tour was coming fast. The night felt bittersweet. I didn't know whether I should worry about the future or just enjoy the wind in my hair and the feel of Jax's callused hands brushing against mine.

Before I knew it, Bernie was pulling to a stop in front of a non-descript, dark building with black walls and a thick oak door. "Here we are," he said, his grin as white as his hair. "You two kids text me when you need to be picked up. I'll park somewhere close."

Jax's eyes narrowed. "I'm not even sure where we—"

"Thanks, Bernie," I said quickly, getting out of the car and extending a hand to Jax. "C'mon, let's go. Didn't I tell you to trust me?"

He arched his scarred eyebrow at me, as if to say, *I'm not so sure about this*, but he took my hand anyway. We walked together to the big oak door, and Jax pulled it open—

To reveal total darkness.

"I think there's been a mistake," Jax said quickly, closing the door again. "They must be closed. The door's open, but it's dark in there."

I smirked. "Just go in anyway. Remember that night you blindfolded me?"

A wry half-smile spread to the corners of Jax's lips. "They say payback's a bitch."

"I thought they said turnabout was fair play. So get in there!"

"Yes, *ma'am*," Jax said, his eyes crinkling with amusement as he stepped inside. I followed close behind.

When the door closed behind us, it was darker than I'd have thought possible. No light came in through the door, and no windows let in any of the Southern California sun. As I stumbled forward, a woman's voice emerged from the darkness: "Welcome to Opaque," she said, calmly. "Do you have a reservation?"

"Yes. Hewitt, table for two," I said, squinting into the darkness but unable to see even the outlines of her face. I slowly put my hand up in front of my face and realized I couldn't see it either.

"Have you ever dined with us before?" the voice asked.

"Are you still serving even with the lights out?" Jax's voice called out.

"Sounds like a newcomer!" Her reply had the sound of a practiced pitch. "Here at Opaque, we believe that seeing isn't everything. We're a pitch black restaurant: no light fixtures, no windows, no flashlights. When you don't rely on your eyes, your other senses sharpen. I'll get your server in just a moment, and then you'll head to your table."

"Huh," Jax's voice floated toward me. "Total darkness. I guess they don't have to worry too much about presentation."

"And more importantly," I said, "welcome to the one place we can eat in Los Angeles without your face ending up splashed on every tabloid in town."

He snorted appreciatively. "Good point." I glowed inside—my idea had worked perfectly, and I'd thought of it completely on my own while going crazy from the downtime. I had another surprise in store for Jax, but I planned to save that one for later in the evening.

Another voice emerged from the black emptiness in front of us. "Welcome," the deep, masculine baritone said. "I'll be your server tonight. Follow me this way—most guests prefer to put a hand on my shoulder so I can lead them to their table."

Jax sounded a little annoyed. "Can't we just follow your voice?"

"That's . . . not usually wise, sir. You could trip if you go off-course. We definitely advise holding on."

"Fair enough." I heard the sound of a hand touching the fabric of the waiter's shoulder, and I reached out until I felt Jax's arm. Making our way across the dark space with small, hesitant steps, we both breathed an audible sigh of relief when the waiter came to a stop and gently guided our hands to chairs.

Sitting down, I once again tried waving my hand to see if I could see an outline. Nothing. *They really weren't kidding about the pitch black part.* I'd somehow thought that I might be able to at least see where Jax was, but only the sound of his breath reassured me that he was there.

"I wonder how the waiters get around," Jax said. "Are they wearing night-vision goggles or something?"

I reached out on the table, searching for his hands. "They're actually blind," I said, sliding my fingers around his. "I looked this up the other day. The restaurant found out that sighted waiters kept spilling, making mistakes—they couldn't get used to it no matter how long they tried. People who were blind from birth did just fine."

"Huh," said Jax, sounding thoughtful. "Makes sense, in a way. For people who can see, there's a loss of control from darkness. But blind people have learned how to control the darkness—how to harness it so it's not a disability."

"When I was a kid, this would have been my nightmare," I said ruefully. "I was terrified of the dark."

"It's pretty weird how kids are afraid of the dark, isn't it?"

"Weird?" I said, confused. "I don't know. I've always figured it was just one of those primal fear things. You know, like, caveman stuff. Fire good, dark bad."

"But we all start in the dark," Jax said, his voice quiet and thoughtful. "We start where it's dark and warm and protected. When we see the light for the first time, we're so scared we cry."

I blinked in the darkness. Was Jax talking about babies? A mental image flashed in front of me: Jax holding a newborn, his scarred brow raised to make a googly face. My heart started beating just a little faster, and I wished I could see the expression on Jax's face. Without it, I had no idea what he was feeling—I felt in the dark, in more ways than one. Was he thinking about the future, or just making conversation?

"So why do you think a newborn is scared of the light, but a three year old is scared of the dark?" I asked, curious about his answer. It seemed like the darkness had loosened his tongue, and after the last few days I was glad to hear him get lost in thought.

"I think it starts when—"

The waiter's voice interrupted us. "I've brought your first course of the evening. Your place settings are in their normal places in front of you, forks on the left, spoons on the right. No knives—liability reasons."

Jax and I laughed nervously, but he continued: "Many people find that eating with utensils is difficult in the dark. All our dishes may also be eaten as finger food if you wish.

Keep in mind that no one will be able to see you eating with your fingers—it can be your secret."

I could hear dishware and glasses clinking onto the table, and feel the cool breezes as servers set our dishes down, but without any visual aids, it was impossible to tell what had been put on the table in front of us. "This is kind of exciting," I whispered to Jax.

"Bon apetit," the waiter said, and his footsteps moved quickly away.

I felt around the table for my fork, found the handle, and then extended my fingers until they were touching my plate. Probing gently with a finger to find where the food was, I suddenly found my fingertip sticking to what felt like a spider's web.

"I think I found it," I said, picking up the spider's web with my fork. It was heavy, I could tell, with something inside it that was soft and yielding. My fingers were still sticky from the web.

From across the table, I heard Jax's fork clink against the plate. "What the hell *is* that?" he muttered.

"Your guess is as good as mine," I said, holding the fork out with trepidation. I'd never eaten a spider's web before, and not knowing what was inside it made me feel almost queasy.

"Okay," he says, "We'll be brave together. On three, got it?"

"Got it."

"One . . . two . . ."

"Three!" I said, and tried to take a bite—only to have the fork sideswipe my cheek.

Jax laughed. "Wait," I said, confused. "How did you see that?"

"See what? I just missed my mouth with the fork and started laughing at myself."

I smiled ruefully. "I can see what the waiter meant about using our hands. But whatever it is, I'm not sure I want to touch it." Thinking for a moment, I had another idea: "Maybe if we're really careful, and feel out where the other person's mouth is, first, we can feed each other."

Jax sounded dubious. "I'm not sure that'll work, but we can give it a try. Just watch out for the eyes, okay?"

I laughed and felt across the table until I found Jax's face. I knew every contour of it, every detail, and as soon as I touched him it was almost like I could see him again. Lingering for a moment with my hand on his cheek, I brought up the bite of spider web, swiping it against his lip, and felt his mouth close around the fork.

I slid the fork away, and he chewed in the darkness. "I . . . huh," he said, after a long pause. "This can't be what I think it is."

"What do you think it is?"

"Try it." All at once, I felt Jax's hand on my face, then the spider web brushing against it, smelling faintly of flowers. There was no time to be squeamish—I bit down on the web.

Instantly, my lips were coated in a sweet, citrusy flavor, followed by a distinct creamy meatiness melting against my tongue. "Oh my god," I said, taking a second bite from the fork in front of me. "What is that?"

The waiter's voice was suddenly nearby. "That is a foie gras medallion enclosed in Earl Grey cotton candy," he said smoothly.

"Almost like a dessert," I whispered. The unexpectedness of the combination was perfect.

"Let me feed the rest of it to you," Jax's voice purred softly, and my lips parted to let the morsel in. Melting, sensuous, the foie gras started to make me feel urges to do things in the dark that we'd gone without for far too long.

The waiter cleared his throat, and I suddenly felt myself blushing. Did the blind waiters' heightened perception apply to my imagination, too? "We have here your entrées," he said. "Be careful, you may wish to eat this with your hands, rather than utensils."

I reached out toward my place setting, and felt dried petals, a whole dried flower, then another and another. *Roses?* When I moved my fingers further, they brushed more petals—these ones wet and smooth. Jax let out a short laugh of appreciation. "Maybe that's why it happens," he said, sounding bemused.

"Why what happens?"

"Why the dark scares us once we're older. We learn to fear the unknown, to think that it's out to get us somehow." His voice was intense, lost in thought. "It's been a long time since I've had to think of food as an unknown. I think I like this place."

"How do you know so much about food, anyway?"I asked. "I'm assuming it's because rock stars get the royal treatment more often than accountants."

"You want the truth?" He chewed for a moment, then swallowed. "I worked in kitchens when I ran away from home. They were the only place I could get work as a scrawny kid with no ID. I tried to learn everything I could. Especially from this one guy, my friend, who kind of took me under his wing. If he'd had his way, I'd be a chef right now."

His answer wasn't at all what I'd expected—and more than that, I was surprised to hear him talking so freely about his childhood. Was it the darkness that was making him more open? "Why didn't you?"

"Sky, mostly," he admitted quietly. "After we started playing music, she wanted to start a band, and that kind of became my life. I still worked enough at the restaurant to make the money I needed, and I kept learning, but I just couldn't put in the hours to learn what I should to run my own kitchen."

I was glad it was dark so Jax couldn't see how shocked his openness was leaving me. We'd come so far together, but there was still so much I didn't know about him. Maybe this was a sign of his growing trust? My heart warmed at the thought.

I suddenly realized I hadn't eaten a bite of my entrée. Picking up one of the dry roses, I popped it into my mouth, where it dissolved into a crunchy, tangy bitterness. It was fantastic. "Whoa, what are these dry flowers?"

"Pretty sure they're brussels sprouts," Jax said nonchalantly. "Arranged like roses—which is pretty clever. They are flowers, after all."

"Nuh uh," I said, shaking my head even though I knew he couldn't see it. "No way is that a brussels sprout. I've hated brussels sprouts since I was three years old."

"Waiter?" Jax said into the blackness. "What's the flower on our plates?"

"The dry flowers are brussels sprouts, roasted with lemon zest and a jasmine-infused sherry vinegar glaze," he said. "The wet flowers are bison tataki, seared with sesame paste."

"Holy shit," I breathed. "You were right. I liked brussels sprouts and didn't even know it."

"That's the nice thing about the dark," Jax said as I chewed a piece of the bison tataki, savoring the wild flavor. "Sometimes the unknown can surprise you—in a good way."

"Like you," I said, thinking aloud, then quickly put my hand up to my mouth.

"Me?"

"Well, yeah." I bit my lip, still feeling embarrassed by how wrong I'd been about our first impression. "When I was walking to your tour bus, you were an unknown. I figured I'd end up having a sleepless, thankless couple of weeks with an irresponsible, entitled rock star."

"But once you found out we'd already met?"

"To tell you the truth, I thought the same thing."

"And how about now?" Jax's voice was warm, and he stroked soft fingers against my wrist, sending shivers of arousal through my body.

"Now. . ." I thought about what we'd gone through together—the hotel suite in Vegas, the hospital room in

California. I took a deep breath to try and steady myself. "Now I can't imagine letting you go."

Jax's hand clasped around mine tightly. "Who said anything about letting go?"

I held his hand quietly for a moment. "I . . . I know it's not going to be the same in a few days, when the tour's over," I said, trying to keep my voice level and calm. "I'm going back to New York, you're staying here to record your next album. It's just. . ."

"What?" Jax asked, his voice calm and assured. "You know I'll come back to New York, right? I do live there."

"Yeah. I know," I said, struggling for the right words. "It's just—I don't know what's going to happen when I leave."

In the darkness, something brushed against my cheek, and I flinched before realizing it was Jax's hand, caressing my cheek. "You're overthinking it." His voice was warm and relaxed. "It's going to be a few weeks in Los Angeles, and I'll be laying down tracks with the band the whole time. Then I'm going to come back to New York. While I'm gone, we'll talk on the phone and it will be fine."

My heart beat faster. We'd been avoiding talking about our relationship for so long, and I had been so careful about getting my hopes up. "So you're telling me that once you're back, we'll . . ."

" . . . Pick things up where we left off? That's what I'm expecting. Unless you'd be too embarrassed to tell your New York friends that you're slumming it with a guy in a band."

I laughed, relief coursing through my body. "Slumming it? Are you kidding? I'll be telling everyone!" Fumbling for my purse next to the chair, I searched with my fingers for the envelope I'd placed inside just before we'd left the bus.

"Here," I said, placing the square envelope in his hand. "I want you to have this."

"What is it?"

"Just . . . something I've been working on for the last few days. A present."

"It's not going to do me much good to open it in the dark," he said, sounding confused.

"It's not for you to open here," I said quickly. "It's for after the tour. When we're apart."

The envelope rustled and I felt Jax's hand close around mine again. "Thank you, Riley. I'll treasure it—whatever it is."

We shared a silence together as I reveled in the removal of a huge weight I hadn't even realized I had been carrying. I was so glad to be done with our conversation about what would happen between us after the tour. And that Jax sounded so sure about it.

Drunk with warm feelings, I felt a torrent of words escaping from my lips before I could stop them. "I'll miss you so much, Jax. I . . . I love you."

My heart thumped so loudly it almost hurt. A small noise came from Jax's throat. After a long silence, he found my shoulder with his arm and gave it a soft squeeze.

"I think you're incredible," he said softly, caressing my arm. "And now I wonder where our dessert is."

I let out a breath I didn't know I was holding. My cheeks got hot with embarrassment. The darkness had made me feel like Jax was ready to open up, but it was clear there were still locked doors in his heart I couldn't reach.

I pressed my lips together together as we shared an awkward silence. Thankfully, the waiter did come with the dessert quickly, giving me time to think as we ate.

I hadn't meant to do it, but I'd finally told Jax how I felt. If those words were hard for me to say, then I knew how much harder it would be for him. Maybe I had been too fast to say it. I probably had.

But it was done, and even if Jax wouldn't tell me he loved me, he had already given me enough for the night. I knew he wanted to be with me, and if we continued to grow together eventually he would say those words.

# Chapter Twelve

## DOUBTS

The next day, I sat alone on the bus. A tapping noise filled the room.

My fingers flew over the keys of my laptop as I pounded out a status report to Palmer. Other than the sound of my typing, an eerie quiet blanketed the bus. I missed the usual noise of the band, but they were downtown doing a meet and greet with a possible producer for their next album.

I bit my lip and tried to concentrate, but my mind kept slipping back to Jax. Last night, I finally found the courage to talk to him about our future past the tour. Knowing that he wanted to be with me once we were back in New York filled me with a happiness that I hadn't known was possible, even if he hadn't been ready to say he loved me yet. We now had a future—and in time, maybe I would be able to unlock all the secrets of Jax's scarred heart.

I shook my head and hunched over the keyboard, willing away my distracting thoughts so I could hurry and finish my report. Crunching numbers was just one thing I had to do today, and the least important to me.

This morning, Jax had invited me to go along with him to his promo at five o'clock. He had seemed eager to hang out with me, even though he warned me that I might not have that much fun at this promo, which he called "lame."

*Waves* magazine planned to do a spread on up-and-coming leaders of hot bands for next month's issue, and they'd invited Jax to participate. But alone, without the rest of the band. No one liked the idea, but Reed had managed to convince everyone that this kind of free exposure couldn't be passed up. So reluctantly, Jax had agreed to do it.

I glanced at my watch. *Shit.*

It said 4:00. If Jax didn't hurry back soon, we'd be late. Not like that didn't happen all the time in the music business, but apparently this world famous photographer hated tardiness with a passion that bordered on the insane. If we were late, Reed informed us, this guy would cancel the whole gig, and then there would be hell to pay not only from him, but also from the rest of the bands involved.

A loud rumble came from outside, and I snapped my head up to listen. Next I heard a jarring screech. *What the hell?*

I ran to the window and peeked out into Reed's driveway.

To my surprise, Jax sat outside on a growling red motorcycle. He wore sunglasses, and held his phone in his hand, typing into it.

I stared at the beautiful bike. It looked smaller and more streamlined than his black Vincent Shadow. More feminine. Why would he be driving something like that?

My phone chimed. Smiling, I picked it up and read the message from Jax: *Hey baby, check this out.*

I hurried outside to meet him, and he revved the engine proudly as I approached. A loud roar filled my ears and I cupped my hands over them for protection. He smiled and switched it off.

"So what'd you do, trade your bike in for this?" I grinned at him. "It looks kind of girly for you."

Jax laughed, his eyes flashing. "That's good. This one's for you."

My eyes widened. *This is too much, Jax.* "Are you serious?"

"Just for today, that is," he said, swinging his leg over the seat and standing up. "It's a rental."

I exhaled, secretly relieved that he hadn't spent a fortune on me. Expensive presents were the last thing I wanted at a time when our relationship seemed more complicated than ever.

"So you left with the band and returned with a bike?" I asked, grinning.

Jax shrugged. "They all wanted to stay downtown. And then I had the idea to get this." He drew his brows together and frowned. "I thought that since I had to do this stupid photo shoot, we might as well have fun getting there."

My stomach twisted with excitement and a little anxiety as it dawned on me that Jax wanted me to ride this bike today.

As in, right now.

"You think I'm ready to drive alone?" I asked.

"Sure," Jax said, his voice steady. "Everyone starts somewhere."

I slowly ran my fingers down one chrome handlebar, the thought of riding again making me a little nervous. I didn't have much experience other than that one insane night.

*Darrel. Ugh.*

Concentrating on the bike, I shook off the pang of anxiety that always came up when I thought about Jax's dad. This bike looked like it would be fun to drive, and Jax seemed confident that I could. I *did* have the fundamentals down, at least.

When I looked back at Jax, I noticed his furrowed brow had been joined by a new tenseness in his jaw.

I pressed my lips together as I took in his strained expression. Was he stressed out about the promo, or was it something else?

"Hey, what's up?" I asked, my voice tinged with concern.

Jax looked up at me swiftly, and his face darkened for a brief second. Then, in a flash, the gloom was replaced by a smile that seemed less than genuine. "Nothing. But if we don't get a move on, we'll be late."

I peered into his face, but I couldn't figure out what was behind those deep, dark eyes. No matter what, though, he had a good point. Every minute we spent standing around, the probability of making it to the shoot in time dwindled.

"Okay," I said, clapping my hands once as if to say *let's get going*. "But I might not be able to go that fast at first, not until I get used to it."

Jax gave a short nod. "That's okay, as long as you remember that the faster you go, the easier it is to ride."

As he went to get his Shadow out of the trailer, I hopped onto my bike and ran my hands over the clutch and the throttle, trying to recall my muscle memory from the night with Darrel.

The last time I rode a bike, I had been forced into it because we needed to escape from the Reapers and get to safety. The direness of the situation didn't leave me much room to worry about riding a motorcycle for the first time.

Now a wave of doubt swept over me. Would I be able to do it again?

I looked at Jax as he rolled his bike up, feeling self-doubt written all over my face. This time, the smile he gave me was real—and drop dead gorgeous.

I smiled back, feeling a surge of confidence spread through my core. If Jax believed in me, the least I could do was believe in myself. I pressed my knees against the slim, aerodynamic body of the bike, liking the way it seemed almost made for me. I took a deep breath and flexed my fingers on the handlebars. It was okay. I wanted this. I'd do my best and have a damn good time doing it, too.

Jax started his engine, revving it into a thunderous roar.

"Let's go!" he shouted.

I exhaled through pursed lips and started up my bike. *Here goes nothing.*

Jax took off, heading for gate at the end of the long driveway. I twisted the throttle towards me, and the bike jerked forward with sudden speed.

The acceleration made me wobble, and I clutched the handlebars, hard.

I remembered Jax's advice, and twisted the throttle again, pumping more gas into the hungry engine. To my relief, I straightened out immediately, and the motorcycle steadied between my thighs.

After that, I didn't wobble anymore, and I followed Jax to the highway, proud of how I could handle the bike.

But as I started to merge onto the busy LA freeway, the cars zoomed by like fighter jets. The late afternoon traffic was faster, meaner, and more intense than the night I drove

Jax's bike. I sent up a silent prayer that I wouldn't get squashed.

Taking a deep breath to steady myself, I concentrated on following Jax. He pulled ahead of me and changed lanes, speeding to pass a slow car. I bit my lip. I didn't want to lose my guide by hanging back.

Gritting my teeth, I jammed on my throttle. My bike zoomed forward, and I swerved into the left lane. I sailed past the car with a whoosh. *Yeah!*

I laughed as I passed another string of cars. "Eat my dust!" I yelled. Adrenaline rushed through my body. I opened up my mouth wide to whoop.

Something small and black whapped me on the lips. I snapped them shut, startled, then quickly spat a bitter, acrid fragment over my shoulder.

Something bonked off my head. A whine buzzed in my ear, then faded away.

I laughed, realizing what it was. Who knew a major hazard of the road would be getting bugs in the face? Normally, I'd be disgusted, but somehow right now I didn't seem to care. It was hard to think about anything bad with the wind in my face and the sun shining down on me.

I smiled. No wonder Jax loved riding so much.

Jax coaxed more speed out of his bike, pulling away from me again. As he changed lanes, he cut sharply in front of a white sedan. The driver jammed on his brakes. His angry red face leaned out the window as he swore at Jax.

My heart beat faster, the adrenaline mixing with a shot of anxiety. What was Jax doing?

Frowning, I gripped the handlebars tighter and pushed my bike faster, wanting to catch up with him so I could tell him to cool it.

Jax swerved and cut off another car. The driver honked as he slammed on his brakes.

Swearing, I urged my bike forward. Several cars still separated us. *Are you trying to kill us, Jax?*

Ahead of us, clogged traffic forced Jax to slow down. The cars and trucks on all sides hemmed him in with nowhere to go.

He slammed his hands on the handlebars. Then he rammed on his throttle, sending his bike to the right. He threaded his way through the tiny space left between the cars boxing him in the lane.

What I saw next made me gasp.

He dashed into a narrow gap between an SUV and an eighteen-wheeler that was shrinking as the eighteen-wheeler picked up speed.

*Jax, no!*

Hunching over the handlebars, Jax darted past the truck, almost scraping it as he whipped by. With a jerk of his arms, he swerved into the lane in front of the truck and out of sight.

A sharp clang filled the air, followed by the sound of screeching tires.

My chest was suddenly tight with fear.

*Oh god. No. Please.*

An opening between the cars appeared on my right, and I swung into it, my eyes wide as I searched for Jax.

I spotted a rusty blue car pulled over on the side of the road. My stomach squeezed into a hard ball. An accident?

I slowed down to take a look at the car. The driver stood outside and gazed down at his tire, scratching his head. I glanced at the tire. It was missing a hubcap. I looked up, my eyes roaming the grass alongside the car. I couldn't see a smashed motorcycle anywhere.

A shaky laugh emerged from my lips, but my eyes were already scouring the highway for Jax. Where was he?

Up ahead a white delivery van switched lanes, and Jax came into view, riding at a normal speed, in a normal lane.

I released a breath I didn't even remember holding.

I gunned my engine, and the spurt of speed brought me close behind Jax. I stared at his back, my heart troubled. What the hell was he thinking?

As we steered off the highway, I took a deep breath, trying to calm myself.

We parked outside the club. I snapped off my engine and turned to Jax.

He sat on his bike, looking elated, as if adrenaline still coursed through his veins. He glanced at me, and his expression sobered up slightly.

"I can't believe you did that," I said, my voice stunned and my stomach uneasy.

Reaching out, he gave my arm a gentle stroke. "I had it under control."

"If just one thing had gone wrong . . ." I shuddered. "Why take that risk?"

He shook his head. "I didn't plan on it. But lately . . ." he paused, searching for words and coming up short. He gave up and shrugged. "It felt good blowing off some steam."

I remembered his tense face from before the ride. "Because of the photo shoot?" I hesitated, sensing something deeper. "Or because it's the end of the tour?"

He got off his bike, not looking at me. "We talked about it in therapy." He hesitated. "Dr. Feinstein . . ." He trailed off, as if he was unsure of what to say next. "He wanted me to find ways to relax. I usually ride my bike for that."

I dismounted from my bike too, coming around to look up at his face.

His eyes glittered strangely, and an almost palpable wave of jittery energy radiated from his body. He didn't look relaxed to me. He almost looked high. I didn't know what to make of it.

I took his hand. "You really scared me," I said simply, fighting back a tear. For a moment, I'd thought that I had lost him.

His scarred eyebrow waggled. "I thought the thrill might do us both some good. I'm sorry I miscalculated. Let me make it up to you?" He bent me down for an exaggerated, Hollywood-style kiss.

As usual, my body responded to his touch. Warm waves of pleasure radiated from my core as his lips probed mine. But when he let me up, I poked him in the side. "Letting off steam is one thing, but taking risks like that . . . I don't know how to feel about you doing stuff like that."

He sighed. "It's nothing to get worried about, Pepper."

"Just take it easy in the future, will you?" I asked with a weak smile, but part of me wasn't joking at all.

"You got it." Jax pulled his phone out of his pocket and glanced at it. "Shit, we've got to go." He looked at me, his eyes still glittering. "Alright?"

I nodded, but I couldn't erase the knot in my stomach as he took my hand. Sky had told me he used to take death-defying risks before he found music, but I thought that was all over now. So what was going on with him?

Was he trying to kill us? Trying to sabotage our relationship? I didn't know what was going on in Jax's head or how to fix it, but everything was definitely not alright.

# Chapter Thirteen

## TAKE CARE

Jax's disdain for the photo shoot made me expect it to be lame, but I couldn't have been more wrong.

We made it just in the nick of time, and only received a short scolding from the photographer, who looked like a slightly plumper Woody Allen. Suddenly, Jax vanished into a flurry of activity and camera flashes. He looked incredible as he posed, taut muscles rippling beneath artfully torn clothing that looked about two seconds from falling off. The shots the photographer was taking wouldn't just be great promotional material, they'd also be tacked up in thousands of dorm rooms and lockers across the country.

For me, the time crawled to a standstill as I waited in a booth in a corner of the club, my mind returning over and over again to the flash of Jax's motorcycle disappearing from my view. His nonchalant attitude didn't reassure me. On the contrary, I felt more worried about him than ever.

I'd already seen how his moods could get out of control. The thousands of dollars in smashed guitars was proof enough of that. Now Sky's story kept echoing around in my head. Jax had been this way before. What was stopping him from turning to risk-taking again?

In spite of my fears, the trip back was completely uneventful. Anyone seeing Jax on his bike this time around would have thought he was a model rider. There was no trace of the reckless, foolhardy biker who had practically dared a truck to splatter him across I-5. But at some point, he might put himself in danger he couldn't get out of—and I had no idea how I could stop him.

As we boarded the bus, a muffled thumping floated down from the second floor, followed by a rhythmic twang.

I cocked my head to listen. The sound of Chewie's practice pads and Kev's guitar meant that the rest of the band had come back from downtown and wanted to catch up on practice too.

Jax kissed me and headed upstairs to the Fortress of Solitude. Knowing he'd probably be busy practicing for hours, I got out my phone and scrolled through the contacts.

*Just call Jen. She'll know what to do. Or at least she'll be able to give you a hell of a pep talk.*

I dialed her number. It rang once, and immediately I heard her voice. "This is Jen, I can't come to the phone right now..."

*Damn it.* Really what I wanted to do was talk to Sky, but if she was practicing, I was on my own. Maybe Kristen could help. Even though she'd never met Jax, at least I could air out my worries. She could tell me I was making a big deal over nothing, and then I'd feel better.

But she wasn't there, either—and I didn't feel like pouring out my troubles to voicemail.

Sighing, I headed up to the rooftop deck. If my friends weren't around, I'd have to tell my troubles to a nice stiff drink as the sun set. At least with the band practicing, the deck was all mine.

When I opened the roof door, I blinked in surprise.

A purple mat lay on the deck floor. Sky lay on her stomach, her back arched as she stretched her arms backwards to grasp her ankles. Her face showed signs of strain, but as she caught my eye she gave me a quick smile.

"Oh, sorry," I murmured.

"No, it's okay," she said, sounding a little out of breath. She released her legs and eased them down onto the mat. "I've done enough poses for today."

"I thought you were practicing with the guys," I said, smiling a bit at my good fortune. It looked like I'd be able to get this load off my chest after all.

Sky stood up and stretched, then grabbed a towel that hung from one of the barstools. "Sometimes I'd rather do this than practice. It gets me loose."

I joined her at the bar. Picking up a bottle of rum, I swished around its contents. "This stuff works better than yoga for that. Care to join me?"

"Sure," she replied, rubbing the towel over her neck. "But make mine a small one. I've hardly eaten all day."

As I mixed fruit juice with the rum in two glasses, I snuck a furtive glance at Sky. Even though we were cordial, we didn't have the kind of friendship that allowed for much talk about Jax's inner life. We didn't talk about Jax at all, usually. But she'd known Jax for forever, and if anyone could make sense of Jax's erratic behavior, it was her.

I handed her the drink. "Here you go," I said, taking a sip of my own while I tried to figure out what to say.

Sky sat down next to me, the towel draped around her shoulders. "I'm glad you came up," she said, taking a sip from her glass. "Actually, I had a question for you." She paused, looking nervous as she waited for a response.

I lifted my eyebrow and smiled, even though her hesitation put me on alert. "Go for it," I said.

She exhaled and shifted on her barstool. "What's going to happen with you and Jax after the end of the tour?"

The irony of it struck me, and I laughed, even though her question wasn't funny. She gave me a confused look and I hurried to explain. "It's funny you should ask. I wanted to talk to you about Jax too," I said. "I didn't know how to bring it up though."

"Me either!" Sky said, a relieved smile appearing on her face.

I wiped my eyes with the back of my hand as I tried to organize my thoughts. I wished I could tell her I knew exactly what would happen with me and Jax, but the truth was, I didn't know. I trusted that he meant what he said about staying together, but who knew what could happen to upset our plans?

"We're going to make it work long distance until he gets back to New York," I said, trying to sound more confident than I felt. "We're committed to making this happen, even though it'll be hard."

Sky's eyes lit up at my words. "That's great, Riley. You've made such a difference in his life." Her face grew serious again. "I mean it. When he's with you . . . I've never seen him happier. Except for lately, but I'm sure that's nothing."

I frowned at the last part. "What do you mean?"

Sky looked embarrassed. "Well, after his collapse, I mean. He gets better, but then he gets worse. For a while I thought nothing could get through to him. But you did it before. I'm sure you'll do it again. It'll just take time."

I gave her a stiff smile. Though her words were meant to be comforting, they struck at the very heart of my worries. What would happen to Jax after I left? Therapy had improved his mood on the surface, but after what I'd seen today, I couldn't take any comfort in it. Something deeper was clearly at work. What if therapy wasn't really helping? And in a few days, if he took a turn for the worse again, he'd be alone.

"So do you think he's getting better?" I asked, trying hard not to show anxiety on my face.

She gave me a curious look. "Don't you?"

"Yes," I said quickly, fighting back the urge to confess all my worries to her. The thought of just unloading it all was tempting, but gnawing insecurities made me stop. The possibility remained that I'd worked myself up over nothing, and spilling my guts would only worry Sky—and make me look like the world's neediest girlfriend. I could ask what I needed to know without telling her all my fears.

"Actually, I had a question for you too," I said, careful to keep my voice casual. "When you told me that story about Jax going subway surfing and doing other risky stuff, it made me wonder. What did he look like after he did something like that?"

Sky paused to think. "Umm . . . high? I think. Like a junkie," she said, laughing. "After a hit."

Even though the sun warmed the roof, I shivered. I didn't know any drug addicts, but I wasn't naive either. What I'd seen in Jax's strangely excited eyes could be described in just that way.

Sky broke into my reverie. "Why, is something wrong?" she asked, concerned.

"Nothing's wrong," I lied, wishing that I could believe my own words. I didn't want to worry her. I didn't even know if Jax would do anything that risky again. I had no real reason to assume he would. "That story just made me curious, that's all. I'm still trying to get a picture of what Jax was like when he was younger."

She sighed in relief. "Ah, okay."

I hesitated, then touched her shoulder. She swiftly brought her head up to look at me. Even if I couldn't tell her everything, I could still use her help, and ask her to do something for me that would make me feel a tiny bit better about leaving.

"I wanted to ask you something else, too." I hesitated, not sure of how to say it.

Sky tilted her head, waiting.

I exhaled. "Could you look after Jax for me while I'm gone? If he starts acting weird again, and I'm not here . . ." I trailed off, not really sure what I wanted Sky to do. If Jax was trying to distance himself from me, who was to say he wouldn't do the same thing to her?

But she nodded, as if she could read the unsaid message behind my words. "Don't worry. I can be there for him. We may not actually have the same parents, but he's my brother, just as much as Chewie."

A wave of relief rushed through me. I could count on her, I knew it. I didn't have a sister, but if I did, I would want her to be like Sky.

"Thank you," I said, the words almost sticking in my throat.

"It won't be the same without you around," she said, sounding sad. "But we'll be back in New York as soon as we're done cutting our new record."

"I'll be waiting," I said, managing a wry smile. "Not very patiently, but I'll be waiting."

Sky laughed. "But before that can happen, we've got to play our last show." She finished the rest of her drink with a gulp. "And that means I should probably do some real practicing."

She stood up and rolled her yoga mat so that it fit snug under her arm. "It was good talking to you, Riley."

I waved to her as she left. Alone, I stared down into my almost empty glass as if it had the answers I was still seeking.

In my heart, I wanted to believe that Jax had found a way to heal. But if he was trying to escape his pain by going back to his old reckless ways, therapy would be nothing but a temporary bandage over a far deeper, older wound.

Or, on the other hand, therapy could be working perfectly and Jax might be a changed man in a few weeks or months. I sighed, my eyes drifting off over the horizon. Without communication, no couple could last. He wasn't letting me in, and if our relationship had started to seem like it was on the rocks, maybe it was because he wanted it that way.

I knew in my gut that something was wrong with Jax, but I didn't know how to help him heal. Soon, there would be no time left for me to even try.

# Chapter Fourteen

### A LOSS

The next few days were nerve-wracking. Jax went off on rides for hours at a time, not telling me where he was going or when he'd be back. It reminded me of when he'd disappeared and almost missed the show at the Roman. He'd told me later that he'd been thinking about Darrel, and that he had taken that long ride to clear his mind of the terrible memories.

But that was *before* he'd seen Darrel again. Somehow I knew this time was different. *Jax* was different, after what had happened with his dad. And it seemed to me like what he was dealing with had a far stronger grip on him than it ever had before.

This morning, he'd rode away again.

I sat in our bed, idly watching *Die Hard* for the fiftieth time, but even though it was my favorite movie my heart wasn't in it. Jax had been gone for hours now, taking off this morning on his bike. He hadn't said a word to me, he'd just left.

A knock came on the door to Jax's room. It opened, and Sky poked her head in. "Hey. Sorry to interrupt."

I grabbed the remote and paused the movie. "No problem, I'm just killing time until Jax gets here. What's up?"

She frowned. "That's what I wanted to ask you. Did he tell you when he'll be back?"

I just shook my head.

"Hmm." Sky's brow furrowed. "Well, we all have a meeting with Reed up at the house right now. About the Anarchy Fest. We're going to leave a day early to get some extra practice in on the actual stage. And we've got to go over our set list before then, obviously."

"When he gets here, I can tell him that's where you guys are," I offered.

Sky sighed and looked at her watch. "Thanks, Riley. I know I should just trust him to come through, but it's been hard lately."

"He'll be here," I said, injecting false confidence into my voice. He hadn't skipped a practice or meeting since missing the sound check at the Roman, but he'd been acting so erratic lately, anything was possible.

Sky gave me a weak smile and closed the door. I heard stamping and the pneumatic whoosh of the door opening as the band left the bus. Sighing, I turned *Die Hard* back on, but I quickly found myself lost in my own thoughts.

After the discussion I'd had with Sky about Jax's risky behaviors, I'd watched him after every mysterious bike ride for a sign of that same "high" look. While I didn't know exactly why it appeared, I knew it was a look he only got after he'd done something incredibly dangerous. It should have comforted me when he came back looking and acting like himself, but why then did I still feel worried?

A slam came from outside, followed by voices. One belonged to Jax. The sound brought a relieved smile to my face. *Good.* He'd come through after all.

Leaning forward, I lifted the window shade to peek out. What I saw made my happiness vanish.

Jax stood in the driveway, handing a wad of bills to the driver of a yellow cab. His bike was nowhere in sight.

*Where was it?* My heart beat faster. Had Jax been in an accident? If so, why wasn't he at the hospital?

I quickly got up and went downstairs, reaching the first floor just as Jax climbed onto the bus.

My eyes swept over him. His eyebrow rose with its characteristic swagger, and I realized with relief that he looked positively perfect. His clothes weren't ripped or torn, he wasn't limping, and no scrapes or bruises were in sight. There hadn't been an accident—motorcycle crashes didn't leave room for looking like a male model afterward.

Which, of course, left the question of exactly what he'd done with his bike.

"Hi, baby," Jax said, his face drawn into a frown as he reached toward me, pulling me in for a big hug that lasted longer than I expected.

I snuggled into his embrace, but his expression troubled me. My question came out muffled against his chest. "Was there an accident?"

Jax sighed. "No. No accident. Everything's going to be okay."

I looked up, confused. "Well, where's the bike? I saw you leaving on it."

Jax put his hands on my shoulders and gently disengaged from my arms. He took a step back from me, his face still sad. "It's gone."

My mouth fell open. "What . . . why? How?"

Jax's eyes became distant. "I sold it. It was time."

I couldn't believe the words coming out of Jax's mouth. "But you loved that bike."

Jax's lips tightened, and his face went hard. "Doctor's orders. I don't want to talk about it."

Avoiding my gaze, he turned away from me and quickly went into the kitchen. He opened the fridge door and gazed at its contents.

I stared at his back, my heart numb. The bike had been his lifeline, his release. What in the world could the therapist have said to get him to sell it?

I opened my mouth to ask, but Jax interrupted me.

"Hey, want anything for lunch?" He held up some sliced turkey. "I'm making a sandwich." His voice sounded normal, and his outward expression had softened.

But somewhere deep in his eyes, I read his meaning loud and clear: *no more questions.*

"Uh, no," I said, bewildered. My mind grasped for something else to say. "But there's a meeting going on at the house with Reed. The band wants you to drop in."

Jax slapped some turkey on two pieces of bread. "Okay. I'll just bring this over."

I watched as he finished making his sandwich, my mind racing with unasked questions. I'd been uncomfortable when Jax took risks on his bike, but I never in a million years would ask him to sell it. So why would the therapist? I really wanted to know more, but I recognized that look I'd seen in his eyes. I'd felt the same way when I went through therapy. Even a well-meaning person's questions somehow found a way to irritate raw wounds.

Jax gave me a kiss on the cheek and left the bus. I sank slowly down on the couch. I knew that I should be pleased that Jax had started taking therapy seriously, if it'd stop his risk taking. But selling his bike? How could that make him happy? It seemed like going from one extreme to the other, all at once.

I stared off into the distance, frowning. From his gloomy face, I could tell that at least for the moment, Jax wasn't happy about losing his bike at all. But what could I do? I had no choice but to go along with it, even if it felt all wrong.

# Chapter Fifteen

### ANARCHY

Two days later found us in Ventura for the Anarchy Fest, about an hour away from LA, and I for one was glad for the change. For me and for Jax. Something was going on with him that I didn't understand.

At first, I thought his gloominess was just about the bike. But after coming home from his last therapy session, he seemed even more withdrawn than ever, like something was eating him up inside. And it hurt me to watch him suffering, knowing that I couldn't do anything to help.

That's why I hoped the change in venue would be good for him—without his bike, playing music was his only refuge. And he'd be playing for more people at Anarchy Fest than at any other place on the tour. Not all of them would be fans— this festival was too big for that—but the band hoped to make a lot of converts.

And I was excited to see them play again, too. Yet when Jax said this morning that he wanted to go out with a bang for this last show, a strange uneasiness settled over me. His eyes had looked so dark and intense as he said those words—making them almost sound like a farewell.

Now, in the growing dusk of early evening, I stood waiting for the show to start. A thick, skunky smoke settled over my head in hazy clouds.

I eyeballed the guy to my right: in his late thirties, sunglasses, vintage T-shirt. He could have been Chewie's older, more tripped-out brother. A joint the size of a stogie perched between his lips.

If I didn't want to get a contact high, I needed to move. But looking around at the drifting smoke over the Anarchy Fest crowd, I could see it would be pointless. *Everyone* seemed to be either getting high or already there.

I shook my head. *Whatever.* Half the people at outdoor festivals came for the music. The other half came for the party. And that's why I'd joined the crowd this evening, instead of watching the Hitchcocks play from backstage like usual. I'd spent so long torturing myself about Jax that the last thing I wanted to do was spend my last night on the tour watching from backstage. At least out with the pulsing, frantic crowd, I could lose myself.

But as I looked at the belligerent, sweaty faces surrounding the stage, I wondered if I'd made the right choice.

People pressed all around me, their faces sweaty and flushed. A lot of them scowled, and a discontented murmur grew louder and louder as we waited for the band to take the stage. I'd seen shows with bad crowd vibes before. It was going to take a hell of a show to bring these audience members out of their angry funk.

A girl on my right wearing only flimsy sandals hopped from one foot to another. "God, is *this* band going to be late too?"

"Why not?" the guy next to her muttered. "Everyone else has."

The girl grimaced. "This festival sucks. I waited for like two hours to use the port-a-potty, and missed seeing the Death Eagles. Now I'm waiting around for these dicks."

"Yeah, it better be worth it," the guy replied, his face darkening. "I've had enough of this bullshit."

He cupped his hands around his mouth and booed. The girl quickly copied him, and the ugly sound grew as people near us joined in.

I glanced around, dismayed. By now I'd seen my fair share of Hitchcocks shows, and every time the crowds had been ecstatic. This one was anything but. Was Jax's performance going to be enough to change their minds?

I shook my head, trying to clear the negative thoughts from my mind. I didn't want to worry about the show, I wanted to enjoy it. I pushed through the crowd towards the stage, hoping I'd stumble across some real Hitchcocks fans. This was my last chance to see Jax in concert, and I wanted to make it worth remembering. At the very least, I wanted to keep from wondering what was going to happen when it was all over.

I squirmed into a gap between two skinny college guys, trying to force myself through. One of them snarled, and gave me a shove.

Arms flailing, my face pressed into the stinky leather jacket of the guy standing in front of them.

Big and bald, he looked down at me from his massive height, his eyebrows drawn together in a furrow. I pushed myself back and froze as I realized who I bumped into. The guy was a *biker.*

My heart thumped in my chest.

The biker started to turn around towards me.

*Jesus, what is he going to do to me?*

His dark eyes met mine, sending a chill up my spine.

Then suddenly, his eyes softened and he flashed me a warm, friendly smile. He was missing a front tooth.

"You all right, little lady?" he asked, his voice sincere.

I nodded, eyes wide, then quickly glanced at his jacket's insignia. A snarling lion. Not the Reapers' skeleton, thank god.

I sighed and gave him a weak smile back as my heartbeat returned to normal. "Thanks, I'm fine. Just trying to get closer to the stage."

The biker's smile grew wider. "I can help with that." Putting his hand on my shoulder, he threw back his head and bellowed, "Coming through!"

People looked up, startled, then blanched at the sight of my new giant biker friend and moved out of the way. It wasn't much, but it was enough to propel me a few yards closer.

"Thanks," I yelled, as the crowd swallowed me up. I caught a glimpse of his grin before he disappeared from my sight. I shook my head. *That'll teach me to make a snap judgment.*

I scanned the new faces around me, hoping to see some of Jax's fanbase. *Come on. I don't even care if it's a bunch of super bimbos. I just want some company.* Instead, I just saw frowns. The booing that had started farther back now swelled up to the front, and the people around me eagerly took up the complaint.

I brought my fingers up to my temples. The noise was starting to get to me. I'd wanted a distraction but not like this.

A spotlight suddenly snapped on in the middle of the dark stage.

My heart surged as the band strode to their places and picked up their instruments. Maybe now the crowd would shut up. They were about to get *rocked*.

Jax, alone in a pool of purple light, strummed the first notes of "Train Wreck."

The booing quieted, but in the void I heard a strident male voice shouting, "You suck!"

Jax flipped him off, then quickly brought his hand back to his guitar as he bashed out another chord. The crowd roared. All around me, people muttered and scowled, and lots of middle fingers jabbed into the air, returning Jax's sentiment.

Spotlights went up on Chewie, Sky, and Kev as they thundered into the song, their instruments meshing with Jax's to create a chaotic beat.

But my eyes stayed locked on Jax. I'd never seen him like this before.

His lip curled as he slung out the lyrics, and his voice soared over the crowd, whipping them up into a frenzy that was half excitement, half hate. He made vicious thrusts with his guitar, crunching out the chords with a scowl of his own on his face.

All around me, people jumped up and down, their hands in the air, their faces angry. I jumped up and down too, unable to stop myself from being swept up in the crowd's energy. It was like a runaway train—now that the crowd was worked up, there was no stopping them.

Jax fell to his knees, his mouth pulled into a snarl, his fingers whipping a blistering solo out of his guitar. His eyes were defiant as the notes screamed higher and higher.

The sound was hot enough to make my mind melt, but a guy next to me glared at Jax and howled, "Fuck you!"

Sweat poured off Jax's face as he got to his feet. Squeezing his eyes shut, he unleashed a roar of obscenities into the mic, his face contorted.

Chewie, Kev, and Sky exchanged puzzled looks, but continued playing. Then Jax swung into the final chorus, each word sharp and biting, seeming like a dagger aimed at the audience.

*This is freaking amazing!* My chest heaved as I danced up and down. If *that* didn't blow everyone's minds, nothing would.

But as the song screeched to a climactic finish, even more cat-calls and jeers filled the air.

I looked around, uneasy. Even though some people were clapping with excitement, the majority of the folks around me still wore frowns on their faces.

Jax wiped sweat off his forehead and grabbed the mic. "So this is Ventura, huh? It fucking sucks!"

The crowd howled in anger. As the band steered into their second song, a mosh pit started in front of the stage, with people kicking and flailing punches as they shoved each other around.

Even though they were far off, the violence rippled out into the rest of the crowd. People were being stepped on and shoved. A guy's bony elbow hit me on the back of the head. I glared at him, rubbing the sore spot, but he danced on, a one-man mosh pit of his own.

A shout grabbed my attention. A long-haired shirtless guy was trying to haul himself up onto the stage. He got one knee up, then paused to shake his fist. His angry eyes were locked on Jax.

My eyes widened. *What the hell?*

Yellow shirted security men swarmed. Yanking him up onstage, they hustled the guy off to the right and out of sight, with his heels dragging the whole way.

My heart thudded in my chest. This was getting really bad.

As the band continued to play, the mosh pit swarmed the stage. Now I could see lots of yellow shirts on the ground, mixing with the moshers. Security was busy busting heads. I wanted to move back, but the crowd behind me was too packed. I gulped. Wasn't this the way riots started?

A strange scent hit my nose and I sniffed the air. The acrid smell made my heart seize. It wasn't ganja.

It was wood smoke.

Sky's voice screamed out from onstage, clashing with the music of the guitars and drums.

Then I saw it. Fire laced the stage wall on the left, high above the band. The drums faltered and stopped. Chewie stood up, pointing and shouting.

A collective gasp went up from the crowd. All around me, people darted scared looks at each other.

But I couldn't take my eyes away. The fire moved fast, tearing at the wall. Flames licked at the ceiling.

The security team became frantic, yelling at the crowd as they motioned everyone back. I caught a glimpse of Sky's frightened face as Chewie hauled her offstage, Kev right behind them.

Tendrils of fire now twined over half the roof. The crowd surged, and a wave of people shoved into me. I stumbled. Yells and shouts filled my ears.

Then the haunting sound of a lone guitar carried over all the chaos.

My breath caught as I got squeezed in a thick clot of people struggling to flee. I craned my neck, struggling to catch sight of the stage again. A head shifted out of the way, and I saw him.

Jax. Standing alone, guitar in hand, sending note after wailing note into the atmosphere. Above, fire raged.

I screamed.

The tide of people swept me along, forcing me away from the stage. Tortured guitar notes hung in the air.

My stomach twisted in agony. What the hell was going on with him?

"Jax!" I yelled, waving my arms frantically. "You have to get away!"

# Chapter Sixteen

### LOSING IT

**Jax**

*Ten Days Ago*

The nightmares had to stop. That shit had been eating away at me for so long, but after the night I had taken Riley to my old house, they had gotten worse.

A lot worse.

Earlier in the morning, I'd woken up on the deck chair with Riley only to see flames flickering on the ground. Heat singed my arms. Even worse, I'd seen Darrel, lurking in the bushes. The shock and terror didn't last long—just a few seconds—but it was enough. Six in the goddamn morning. I wasn't sleeping after that.

I couldn't stay cooped up on the bus, not after seeing that shit. Fortunately, I had somewhere to go. Reed's house was typical new money Malibu trash, but it had one great feature: it was designed top to bottom with incredible acoustics.

It should have been a perfect way to get through a shitty morning. Music was the only thing that had ever calmed me down when I felt like I was losing it.

A few hours and a pissed off band later, I was sitting alone in Reed's living room, surrounded by smashed guitars. A boiling anger writhed in my chest. The music still wouldn't fucking work.

Nobody else thought the instruments sounded messed up. Which probably meant it wasn't the instruments, it was my head. But that didn't make it any better. If I couldn't blow off some steam with my music, I didn't know what else to do. I was on a hair trigger, and the sour notes had me ready to explode.

Clenching my jaw, I sat in a chair in the practice room and took a fresh guitar from its stand, determined to try again. I tuned each of its strings. They didn't sound perfect, but it was a little better.

With a deep breath, I picked out the opening to "Glass Brick." Nothing. Just a bunch of notes slopped together. Amateur hour. I had a better sound when I was fifteen. Gritting my teeth, I went through the motions of the song, hoping for anything that sounded like fucking *music*.

It wouldn't happen. I played through the first verse, hoping, feeling like I was hitting every chord perfectly, but it still sounded awful. The notes were right, the *sound* was shit. The more I played, the hotter my anger boiled.

Finally, I got to the song's climax, the crescendo building as I played harder and harder just trying to get a few seconds of something that felt good, that felt like my music was supposed to feel. I built it up and poured my heart into every chord.

My jaw clenched as I wrestled out the last note.

Nothing. My stomach twisted. It was shit—all of it.

My anger boiled over and filled me with an unstoppable rage. I grabbed the guitar by its neck, whipped it around, and slammed it to the floor, severing its neck in two. Tossing it aside, I snatched another broken guitar off the floor and hurled it at the wall. Its jagged body snagged on a painting, and with a nasty sound of ripping canvas, fell to the floor.

Fuck.

My chest heaved as I struggled to catch my breath. With a sickening feeling in my gut, I surveyed the wreckage. Broken guitars everywhere. And now a fucked up painting, too. I picked up one of the broken guitars and looked at, but it was pointless. It was too messed up to ever come to life again.

The door flew open and there she was. *Riley*. My heart sank. What the fuck had gotten into me? She was the last person who deserved to see me like this. We'd been through some awful shit together, and she'd stuck by me while being an incredible badass through it all. The last thing I wanted was to burden her with my pain.

Taking a deep breath to try and calm myself down, I tossed the splinters of the guitar against the wall.

I watched her gingerly survey the damage before looking at me with those mischievous, beautiful blue eyes. I knew she was trying to put on a strong face when inside she was scared as hell. That tore me up more than anything else.

"Need any help smashing stuff?" she asked, plunging her hands into her pockets. "I have a pretty good arm."

\*\*\*

*Nine Days Ago*

I'd never been to therapy before, but I needed answers. I was literally losing my mind, and I had to do whatever it took to get better—even if that meant talking about the dark stuff that I normally shut out.

But it was hard. It was the most difficult fucking thing I'd ever done. I'd *never* talked about my dad with anyone except Riley. But Dr. Feinstein didn't push me. He just sat at his desk, listening patiently. I lay on the couch. For some reason, not looking at him while I talked helped. But I hated every minute of it.

For the most part, I concentrated on what had happened that night with Darrel, since that's when my problems started getting out of control. Ever since then, everything had just gotten worse and worse. The nightmares. The flashbacks. My anger. Seeing things that weren't there. My fear that I was losing my mind. By the time I was done, I had a sinking feeling in my stomach.

I lay on the couch, listening to the scratch of Dr. Feinstein's pen on his pad of paper, my stomach sick from having to talk about painful shit I'd tried for years to forget. There was no way this guy was going to help me. I was too fucked up for some feel-good talk to make things any better.

He cleared his throat, and I glanced at him. His eyes looked serious, and I swallowed, hard.

"I know this has been a painful process, Jax. It takes a lot of bravery to open up about your past like you have."

I remained silent. His compliment didn't make me feel better. It just made me more anxious about what he was going to say next. What his diagnosis could be.

He continued, "Good news is, I don't think you're crazy."

I ran a hand through my hair. Was that good?

"When people go through traumatic events like the ones you've described," he replied, sounding sympathetic, "They often have symptoms like yours. Nightmares, mood swings, and especially flashbacks are all indicators. It's common in soldiers—a condition called Post Traumatic Stress Disorder, or PTSD."

My shoulders stiffened. "But I'm not a soldier."

Dr. Feinstein folded his hands across his lap and sat back in his leather chair. "They're just the most commonly afflicted. Anyone who has experienced a life or death situation, where they feel intense fear, horror, and powerlessness, is at risk for PTSD."

"Okay," I said slowly, "And that means . . . what, exactly?"

He spoke slowly and distinctly, his fingers flexing against each other. "For you, your father has all the power. And that's what we need to fix—we want to give the power back to you."

My jaw clenched. "I left home when I was fifteen," I said tersely. "Darrel does not have all the power over me."

He nodded as if to concede the point. "Okay, I may have misspoken. Not all the power. But still, more than you want. Is that fair?"

"I guess."

"Very well. *That* is what we want to fix."

"How?" I asked.

Instead of answering my question, the doctor stayed silent for a moment. I waited with a feeling of impatience. Why wouldn't he just tell me what to do?

He cleared his throat. "When you think about that night, what comes to mind first?"

I frowned. How was this going to make me better? "I try *not* to think about it."

"But when you can't help it?" he continued, his voice gently persistent. "What do you think of first?"

I sighed. "Darrel."

"Good." His pen scratched over paper. "What else?"

I closed my eyes. "Fire."

"Anything else?"

"My bike not starting." My palms began to sweat, and I opened my eyes. "So what? What does it matter what I think about?"

Dr. Feinstein didn't say anything. I clenched my hands. The silence in the room grew.

"Why do you want me to keep thinking about this?" I blurted out. "I don't *want* to think about it any more. That's the whole point. I've been going out of my way to avoid thinking about this shit."

He tilted his head to the side. "And has it been working?"

"No. I told you."

"Why do you think that is? Why can't you forget when you're actively trying to?"

I closed my eyes. "I don't know. Something's getting in the way."

"Right," Dr. Feinstein said, "And what do you think that could be?"

"I don't know, Doc," I groaned, wishing he'd give me answers instead of more questions. Opening my eyes, I stared at the ceiling. "Something is making me remember when I don't want to."

Dr. Feinstein nodded. "It's not just something, Jax. It's more specific than that. Anything you saw that night can trigger an emotional response, like the ones you've been having."

I let that sink in for a minute. The doctor scratched something on his pad, seemingly in no hurry to say anything else.

His pointed silences were beginning to piss me off. "So you're telling me that if I avoid the stuff I saw that night, all this shit will stop?" I asked, unable to keep the irritation out of my voice.

Dr. Feinstein smiled for the first time, and I could tell from the pleased look on his face that I'd hit on something. "The mind can heal itself, but not if it's being aggravated by constant reminders of your trauma. This is where I want you to start. Do you think you can try to avoid all the things that remind you of that night?"

I frowned."Maybe. I mean, Darrel will be easy to avoid. I never want to see that bastard again."

"What about fire?" Dr. Feinstein asked, his calm voice urging me on. "Can you do something about that?"

An uneasiness settled in my gut, and I rubbed my hands together. "That could be a problem. We use pyrotechnics for our shows."

"Are they necessary?"

"They're for the fans," I said, raising an eyebrow at him. From his buttoned up appearance, it didn't seem like Dr. Feinstein had been to any concerts in awhile. He wouldn't be asking if he had. "They pay to see a rock show, we give it to them."

He inclined his head, acknowledging my reluctance. "I can see how that would be hard, then. But I think it's an important step in getting better."

I sighed and leaned back on the couch, suddenly exhausted. "Okay. I'll look into it."

Dr. Feinstein cleared his throat again. "What about your bike? Do you use it all the time?"

"Yeah, I do," I said, the uneasiness deepening in my gut. I glanced at the doctor, and his serious face just confirmed my fears. "No. My bike is off limits."

He tapped his notepad with his pen. "You're willing to give up the pyrotechnics. What's different about the bike?"

I grimaced and balled up my fists hard until my fingers hurt. "I love my bike. If I didn't have it, I'd be stuck on the bus all the time. Sometimes I just need to be alone, you know? To just blow off steam when things get bad. Get a good rush."

"But if your bike is triggering your symptoms, how will you get better if you keep it around?"

"I don't know," I said rubbing my head with frustration. "That's too much, Doc."

Feinstein gave me an understanding look. "I know it's a lot to ask you to do, but if you want to get better, then unfortunately you'll have to make some sacrifices. It's all part of the process. Remove the triggers, and come in for regular therapy sessions."

I looked at him skeptically.

"If you're committed to getting better, you probably will. I can't make any promises but I've seen many patients have success with this program. Some have had to make big sacrifices in order to get better like leaving their current home because it was the place where they experienced the trauma. But again, you have to follow the program."

A hot spike of anger swirled in my chest. No way my bike was causing all this bullshit. So what if I'd been using it that night? I rode it all the time. Maybe the Doc was right about some of the stuff he was saying, but he was wrong about this.

Dr. Feinstein shifted in his seat as if waiting for my answer.

"I'll work on the fire stuff," I said, my voice curt. "I can't promise anything about the bike yet."

He shook his head, but his face stayed neutral. "I have to warn you, until you find a way to avoid your triggers, you should expect to continue experiencing disturbing episodes. And each episode you have only adds to the trauma that we need to fight against."

I nodded slowly. What he said sounded pretty straight up, but I still didn't buy into the idea that my bike was to blame for my problems. If I had to prove it to him, I would, by cutting the pyros from our act and staying away from fire. That should make me better, and then we could drop all this getting rid of my bike shit.

"I'll see what I can do," I said, my tone flat. He could take it or leave it.

He smiled at me, apparently deciding that I'd agreed with him, then began shuffling papers around on his desk. "We all want you to get better, Jax."

His words made me think of Riley. I was doing this for her, more than I was for me. The way she'd looked so frightened, bending over me after I woke up from my nightmare—I never wanted her to look that way again. Afraid for me. Afraid *of* me.

She wanted me to get better, and I wanted to get better for her. She was the best thing that had ever happened to me—and I wasn't going to lose her now.

*** 

*One Day Ago*

I was back on Feinstein's couch again, and I was pissed.

After twenty minutes of telling him about how I'd followed all of his advice and it still wasn't working, he narrowed his brows and asked me if there was anything else I was missing.

"What do you mean?" I asked, frustrated. "I just told you all the shit I've done and it hasn't helped at all! When is this going to start making a difference?"

Dr. Feinstein studied me from his leather chair. "It will make a difference when you find the trigger that is causing your issues. Do you think there may be anything in your life that you've missed? Think back carefully."

I felt my temper rising and did my best to suppress it. After giving up fire, I hadn't gotten better—and I'd been forced to put his last piece of advice into action. "I sold the damn bike. What else do I have to say? No, there's nothing left. Yes, I still have a nightmare every fucking night."

He scribbled on his pad but said nothing for several seconds. "Have you had any more sleepwalking episodes?"

I sighed and bit my lip hard. This treatment was going nowhere. "No. Is that the most progress I can hope for? I'm hallucinating, Doc. This isn't working."

Dr. Feinstein wrote something on his pad and then put the pad down and rubbed his eyes. "Jax, I want you to think very carefully back to that night. Think about objects *and* people that you associate with what happened. Can you do that?"

"Doc, we've already done this."

"Can you humor me? Just put your head back on the couch and close your eyes for a moment."

I took a deep breath and did as he asked. "Fine," I said, my eyes closed.

"Thank you. Now tell me what you see."

"Riley and I are on my bike. I'm showing her the trailer park. The biker gang is there, and they're saying shit about Riley. Then Darrel comes out and I'm fighting."

A dull pain made its way down my spine and I opened my eyes and sat up. "Doc, I told you, we've already done this. There's nothing new."

He nodded and scratched some things on his pad, saying nothing. I watched him for several seconds, waiting for an answer, but he wouldn't speak.

As I waited for him, I thought about what he could be scribbling on his notepad. A sinking feeling started in my stomach. No. It couldn't be. I continued to watch him until he stopped writing and then waited for him to speak. He wouldn't.

"What are you writing?" I asked finally, unable to contain myself.

He looked up at me, blinked, and then put his pen down and sat back, observing me.

I clenched my fists in frustration and took a deep breath. So he was playing the silent game, again. He did this every session. I needed to say the right thing to get him to talk.

"Doc," I said quietly, looking at the ground. "Is it Riley? Is she my trigger?"

His face was a mask. He continued to watch me.

"I'm crazy about her," I said quickly, trying to wrap my head around the idea. "We have so many other memories together. So much good stuff from the tour. I don't get how my mind would just focus on that one night. It's stupid. "

This got arched eyebrows from Dr. Feinstein, but that was it.

My stomach rolled over. "I don't know what I'm going to do if she's what's fucking me up. Riley's all I have right now. How could she be the one causing all this?"

Dr. Feinstein scribbled something quickly on his pad and then put the pad down and leaned forward. "Jax, how would you describe your relationship with Riley since the night you aggravated your condition?"

I glared at him but he just stared back. I didn't like where this was going. "I don't know. She's amazing. I don't know how she puts up with my shit sometimes. Especially lately."

"Do you two spend a lot of time together?"

"I guess."

He nodded, but said nothing more. A full minute ticked by, and with each tick I felt more frustration. Finally, I couldn't keep it in anymore.

"You really think she's it, don't you? You think Riley's my trigger."

He looked at his watch. "I think sometimes the answers to these questions are difficult and not at all what we want to hear. I'm sorry, Jax. I know this is very difficult. In any case, that's just about all the time we have today. I think you've made tremendous progress."

My breathing was ragged. "Wait. What do you think I should do?"

He pressed his lips together. "Someone with a condition like yours, in the constant presence of their trigger, is very likely to act erratically."

His words stung like an angry hornet's nest. "So I'm a time bomb?"

He shook his head. "You're not a bomb, Jax. Please don't think about it that way. It isn't healthy."

"Fine," I said, my heart sinking. "Let me ask you point blank: do you think I need to break up with Riley?"

He looked over at the clock again before returning his gaze to mine. "I'm sorry, Jax, but we really are out of time. There are no easy answers for this, and you don't have to decide today. Just be conscious of the consequences of whatever decision you make. For yourself, and for everyone around you."

I looked at him, my stomach a lead weight. He returned my gaze impassively, until I couldn't take it anymore.

I got up and trudged out. What the hell was I going to do now?

\*\*\*

*Forty-five minutes ago*

Anarchy Fest. It was our final show. We were supposed to go out with a bang. But the crowd was angry. And if they were angry, then I was angry. This wasn't a good day to ask me to put up with people's shit.

After some douchebag yelled out "you suck!" as we started our first song, I gave him the middle finger before rocking out on my guitar. The crowd roared, and I tore into the song. I put everything I had into my solo, but I still heard a "fuck you" sail out from the audience.

That fucking did it. I snarled a stream of profanity into my mic and ended the song with a bang. That should've been enough, but I couldn't stop myself.

"So this is Ventura, huh?" I shouted. "It fucking sucks!" The crowd howled with anger. I looked over at Sky, who mouthed "what are you doing" at me. I shrugged and turned my attention back to the mic. After a few clacks from Chewie, we were into the second song.

But then I saw something terrifying. *Fire.*

My palms began to sweat. Fuck, was I hallucinating again? Like the morning after I sleepwalked?

That was when I caught Darrel out of the corner of my eye. He was at the edge of the crowd, and it was only for an instant, but I saw him.

Or thought I saw him? Was I losing my mind?

I blinked and refocused myself on the song, strumming my guitar with vicious strokes. But I could still see fire out of the corner of my eye. I took a deep breath. No way was I letting my fucking PTSD ruin this show by freaking out on stage.

My eyes scanned the crowd and saw a mosh pit developing in the front. To the left, I saw something that scared me.

Riley.

Her eyes were wide with panic and she was pointing at me. At the stage. The crowd around her was totally fired up, churning into a frenzy.

My stomach dropped. *God, Riley, get out of there.*

The heat behind me was blazing. I saw some flames down by my feet.

Sky screamed something at me. Distantly, I heard the rest of the band stop playing. But I couldn't stop. My fingers kept flying across my fretboard, pulling out note after note.

As I played, my eyes flew back up again to where I'd seen Riley. I was just in time to watch her fall in the crowd. She was immediately surrounded by a herd of people. They had their backs to me.

*Wait, what?* My fingers came to a sudden halt.

"Jax!" Sky yelled from somewhere, "Get off the stage! It's burning!"

I swiveled my head over my shoulder and somehow everything snapped back into focus. Fire tore at the ceiling and down the sides of the stage. This was no hallucination. The stage really was on fire.

A sinking feeling shivered through my body. What the hell was going on with me? I shook my head and looked out into the fleeing crowd.

Riley was in there somewhere.

I needed to get to her. With a start, I unslung my guitar from my shoulder before tossing it aside and hopping off the stage. Riley—I couldn't let her get hurt. Gritting my teeth, I forced my way through the crowd. If I lost her, I'd lose everything.

***

*Five minutes ago*

My heart thundered in my chest as I scanned the area frantically. She wasn't there.

It had taken me a few minutes to shove my way through the crowd to where Riley had fallen, and by the time I had gotten there she was gone.

Now I didn't know what to do.

In a panic, I made my way toward a security guy in a yellow jacket.

I grabbed his arm. "I saw someone fall when I was on stage. Have you seen her?"

The security guy tore his arm away from my grip. He opened his mouth, probably to tell me to fuck off, but something in my face made him stop. "Strawberry blonde?" he said gruffly. "Yeah. She should be headed to the medical tent."

"Is she hurt?" I asked breathlessly.

He shrugged. "Don't think so."

Without another word I turned and began making my way to the medical tent. With the huge crowd of people to fight my way through, it took me twenty minutes to get there. Every minute of it was pure torture. What if that guard was wrong and Riley was seriously hurt? If she was, it was all my fucking fault.

My brain went into overdrive as I walked. I needed to get myself together. Pissing off that crowd, knowing in the back of my mind that Riley was there, had been stupid. Idiotic. Insane.

Why did I keep doing all these fucked up things?

My head felt like it was tied loosely to my body. What if the next thing I did was something even worse? Who would get hurt?

A chill went through me. This was it. I was losing my mind. Going crazy. Or something. How would I know?

Fuck.

I approached the medical tent feeling like I had a gun to my head. Something had to change. If I kept going like this, the next crazy thing I did might be something I'd regret for the rest of my fucked up life.

# Chapter Seventeen

## DISORIENTATION

**Riley**

When I fell in the crowd, I thought I was going to die.

It was a minute that felt like an eternity. I caught a few kicks as people stumbled over my prone body, but thankfully no one stepped on me before a security guard cleared people away so I could stand up.

My eyes flew to the burning stage, but it stood empty, with Jax nowhere to be seen. I grabbed the security guard and asked if he'd seen Jax leave the stage, but he said he'd been too busy handling the crowd to notice. I stood there, not knowing what to do. The security guy kept urging me to go to the medical tent, and in my dazed mind, a light went on—maybe they'd taken Jax there too.

The security guy led the way to the big white tent that stood near the entrance gate. Inside, I looked around but couldn't see Jax anywhere. I quickly asked an older guy with gray hair who seemed to be in charge whether anyone had seen Jax. When he said no, my stomach churned. Was he okay? Or was he lying in an ambulance somewhere?

A nurse had me sit down on a cot. As she patched up a scrape on my arm, I tapped my feet impatiently against the floor, desperation growing in my chest. Watching him stand on that burning stage had been horrible—but not knowing what had happened to him after was even worse.

As soon as the nurse finished, I jumped up and hurried to the exit. I stepped out into the fresh air and paused, unsure of where to look for him next.

Then I heard Jax's voice shouting "Riley!" His voice came from somewhere on my left.

I turned around, my heart beating wildly.

There he was, making his way through the crowd of people. An overwhelming sense of relief washed over me. He hurried across the grassy area separating us, and my eyes raked over him, looking for signs of hurt. But except for a smudge of soot on his cheek and a cut on his hand, he seemed okay in spite of what had just happened.

When he drew near, he pulled me into his arms for a bone-crushing hug. "Are you okay?" he asked desperately. "Tell me you're okay."

"I'm fine," I gasped, running my hands along his back. "Are you?"

The muscles in his shoulders tensed underneath my fingers, as if he had just remembered something. "Yes," he muttered, pulling away from me.

"God, I'm so glad," I said, reluctantly letting go of him.

He didn't say anything, and kept his eyes cast on the ground. His shoulders slumped. I looked at him intently.

"Jax," I said, my voice tinged with concern, "What happened out there?"

He winced and took a step back, furthering the distance between us. When he lifted his eyes to mine, his haunted expression shocked me. "I don't want to talk about it," he said, his voice hoarse.

My heart thudded in my chest. Something was wrong. How could there not be, when he'd stayed on that stage, playing his guitar as everything burned all around him?

And whatever was wrong, this wasn't the place to deal with it. Not surrounded by all these people. "What if we went back to the bus?" I rushed out. "Maybe you'll feel better there. We can be alone."

His mouth set in a thin line, like he was suppressing some kind of hurt, for what seemed like a long time before he finally nodded. A deep uneasiness settled in my chest. Instinctively I reached out and took his hand, not sure of who I wanted to comfort more—him or me. He hesitated, then his fingers curled around mine in a tight grip. A flash of his old tenderness awoke in his eyes.

But then it was gone, and his eyes filled with pain again. Swallowing, I kept his hand wrapped tightly in mine as we made our way through the throngs of people.

We walked together through the fairgrounds in silence, each lost in our own thoughts. Every now and then I caught a glimpse of his anguished eyes resting on mine and a pain shot through my heart. He hadn't always been this way, not when I'd first met him—he'd been troubled, sure, but not this dark. Never this dark.

When we got back to the bus, I followed Jax into the common area and sat down nervously. He stayed standing, eventually beginning to pace up and down the bus, clenching and unclenching his fists. His eyes were distant and unfocused, as if he was trying to untie a knot in his mind.

As he paced, my anxiety grew.

"What is it?" I blurted out, unable to bear the sight of him in pain any longer. "Please talk to me."

He stopped, and gave me a look that was part fear, part misery. "I don't know what to do," he said, his voice wracked with anguish.

A chill wrapped around my spine. His face was wild in a way I'd never seen before. Why was he looking at me like that? "You're scaring me," I said. "Tell me what's wrong."

He ran a hand through his hair, his eyes widening. "When I saw you fall . . ." He stopped, his jaw clenching. "You could've been hurt," he went on, a tortured look on his face. "And it was my fault. All mine."

I stared at him. "How was that your fault? You didn't knock me over."

He shook his head. "No. Before that. The crowd was pissed and I just gave it right back to them and made it worse. And you were in there!" He grimaced. "I'm just . . . I'm not thinking right, Riley."

He began pacing again with quick, agitated movements, as if by doing so he could escape whatever tormented him.

I watched him with uneasy eyes. "This was a one time thing, Jax. And I'm fine."

He pressed his hands to his temples. "It's not just one time!" he groaned. "This has *been* happening. It will keep on happening."

My heart sank at the frustration in his voice. "We don't know that."

"*I* know that!" he shouted, his eyes wide with panic. "You're not safe around me."

The conviction in his voice scared me, even more than the tortured intensity in his eyes. "Jax," I pleaded, "Stop."

My words bounced off of him, not slowing him down for a second as he kept on pacing up and down the room. "Why do you keep putting up with my shit?" he growled, glancing at where I sat huddled on the couch.

"You know why," I said, my voice unsteady.

That made him stop in mid-step. "Yeah," he said, his voice dropping lower. "I know." His jaw worked as he struggled to find more words. "That's what makes this so fucked."

The oppressive weight in my chest grew heavier. "What do you mean?"

A pained expression flashed across his face, then he lowered himself slowly to sit next to me, his mouth set in a grim line. Reaching out, he touched my hand for a second, then looked down at the floor. It was a moment before he spoke. "I don't know if I can do this anymore," he said in a quiet voice.

My stomach clenched with a sudden sickness. "No," I cried, "You can't mean that. Not now."

His shoulders hunched, and he rocked forward, still not looking at me. "I don't know, Riley. I don't know what to think about anything anymore." He picked his head up swiftly, and his desperate gaze pierced me to my core. "But I can't see you get hurt, and I don't think I can promise you that won't happen."

Tears welled up in my eyes. "But why? I don't understand. Why can't we fix this?"

His jaw tightened, and the stubborn look in his eyes was one I knew all too well. "This isn't something you can fix."

"So it's a problem with me, then?" I said in a small voice. "I did my best to be there for you, Jax."

He winced. "No, it's not you . . . but it is. Fuck, this is so fucked up!" He slammed his hand against the couch.

A fresh wound ripped open in my heart. So that was it— he just didn't want to be with me anymore. "So it's me," I said, grimacing with pain.

His eyes widened. "No, Riley, I didn't mean that. Not that way. You're the best girlfriend, everything I ever wanted. Everything I never dreamed I'd have." He stopped, his voice choking. "You've been so good to me. God knows I haven't deserved it."

I looked up at him, and read the truth in his eyes, and in the firm line of his lips. My head swam with confusion. "Then *why*?"

He closed his eyes. When he opened them again, he looked defeated. Hopeless. "I have PTSD, Riley." His voice sounded bitter. "Post traumatic stress. From that night with Darrel."

My eyes widened, and I pressed my lips together, unable to speak as my mind reeled. PTSD, like the Iraq War vets got sometimes. Of course—it all made sense now. Since that night with Darrel, he'd been acting totally differently. Like someone still trapped in hell.

I dashed away a tear, a small sensation of hope growing in my chest. At least now I knew what we were fighting against. "But that's something you can get better from, right?"

He nodded, but defeat still hung around his slumped shoulders.

I touched his arm, making him turn and look at me. I gazed deep into his eyes, searching in their wounded depths for some way to make this right. "Then why not let me help you? Why are you doing this to me? To *us*?"

He exhaled a shaky breath. "I don't want to!" he cried. "But you've been with me the past few weeks, you know what it's like! I can't control myself. Damn it, I'm even seeing things that aren't there! I'm sick. And if you get hurt . . ." He trailed off with a wince. As if of all the things that had ever hurt him, that would be the worst.

I gripped his arm as anger suddenly flared in my chest. This was all Darrel's fault. I couldn't let the pain he'd caused drive us apart—I just couldn't. "I don't care if you hurt me," I said with heat in my voice.

He rubbed his forehead. "How can you say that? After all I've put you through?" His mouth drew down into a grimace that frightened me with its determination. "No, Riley. This has to end."

My heart wrenched, and I shook my head stubbornly. "I'll do whatever you need. You know that." My lip trembled. "Just don't push me away."

"You can't help me with this," he said, his voice rising in frustration. "Even the doctor thinks so."

"What?" I cried, my voice sharp. "What does he know?"

He scowled, as if he were angry at what he had just said. "Forget it."

My grip tightened on his arm. "No, Jax. I want to know. What does the doctor say?"

His scowl deepened. "My PTSD. He thinks since you were there that night, that seeing you triggers all my symptoms. He already had me get rid of my bike. And now . . ." He hung his head.

The full weight of his words hit me like a punch in the stomach. "God, no. He wants you to get rid of me?"

He didn't look at me. "Yes. And I'm starting to agree."

His words shook me to my core, sending a deep hurt pulsating through my entire being. I was the one causing him pain? All this time? A shudder wracked my body. "No," I managed to get out. "No matter what the doctor says, I can't believe that you want this."

He brought his head up, giving me a piercing look that told me everything about the agony every hurtful word was costing him. "It's killing me," he said, his voice rasping.

"Then there has to be another way," I cried.

The desperation that sprung in his eyes made me shiver. "But don't you see?" he said, his voice dropping lower, "I don't care if you're triggering all this shit. I would live with PTSD forever if I could just have you. But you're going to get hurt. And if there's one thing I can control about this shitty situation, then I'm going to do it. I'm going to make sure you're safe."

My throat choked as tears streamed down my face. He had it backwards—the only place I'd ever felt safe was with him. "This isn't right. You know it isn't. I love you."

He pressed his hands to his forehead, as if those three words had cut him deeper than any wound he'd ever revealed to me in our time together. "Riley, don't. You're making this harder than it has to be. Please."

I shook my head as a sob caught in my throat. "I won't give up on us. Not now. Not ever. You mean everything to me."

Closing his eyes for a moment, he pressed his lips together. His shoulders shook as he took a deep, shuddering breath. Then he sat up straight, opening his eyes and giving me a look that almost broke me with the intensity of his anguish—for what we had together, and for what we were about to lose.

"You mean everything to me too," he said, reaching out to stroke my cheek. His touch electrified me, as it always did, even through my sadness. None of it made any sense. How could he let go of what we had together?

I brought my own hand up to his, and pressed it to my cheek, holding him there. Keeping him with me.

His tortured eyes looked deep into mine, piercing my soul. "But don't you see—" He bit off his words, his brows drawing together as frustration struggled across his face.

I looked at him, my eyes filled with mute appeal. My hand clasped tighter on the warmth of his. *Please, Jax. Don't do this.*

Suddenly, Jax tore his hand away like I'd burned him, a scowl forming on his face. I couldn't tell if he was angry at me, or at himself, but another stab of hurt rocked my body nevertheless.

With an abrupt movement, he stood up. "Fuck. I have to get out of here. I can't do this right now."

I leaned towards him, every fiber of my being aching with the need to be near him. "Stay, Jax. Please."

He clenched his hands, frustration still hanging over his dark brows. "No. I've . . . I've got to go find the band. You should rest. If you need me later, I'll be sleeping on the deck tonight."

"I want to talk about this more," I said, my voice trembling.

"I'm sorry, Riley. But I can't." He turned and walked away from me. Each step he took was like a spike through my heart.

At the door though, he paused. "See you in the morning," he said. His voice was so soft I almost didn't hear him.

Then, with one last anguished look at me, he left the bus. I sank back down on the couch, overwhelmed and heartsick.

*Is this really how it ends?* I didn't want to believe it, I *couldn't* believe it. But what if I really was bad for Jax? I'd been afraid of this before, because I was the one whose insecurities had led us into our run in with Darrel in the first place. And now Darrel—and the pain he'd caused—was tearing us apart.

My heart pounded painfully in my chest. Was it too late for us? It seemed like I was making everything worse for Jax, when all I ever wanted was to make things better. But even so, I didn't want to lie down without a fight. If I did, then Darrel would win—and that was an injustice that neither Jax or I should have to live with.

No matter what he said, I still felt like he wanted to be with me. Even if he'd never told me he loved me, I saw in his eyes how much he cared for me, every time he turned his dark gaze to mine. I could feel it in his tenderness every time we touched.

And I wanted to be with him. Mind, body, and soul. I couldn't give up on us, not now. We had come too far, fought too hard for what we shared—a trust, a desire, a comfort like no other.

In a daze, I went up to the Fortress of Solitude and sat down on the bed, my mind a jumble. If we could work together, and believe in our trust for each other, we might still have a chance.

# Chapter Eighteen

### BURNOUT

I woke up alone in Jax's bed. For a brief second, everything seemed fine. Then I remembered, and the realization that Jax and I were on the rocks hit me like a ton of bricks. Being awake physically hurt.

I sat up in bed and rubbed my eyes, remembering my resolution from last night. I couldn't let us be defeated, not yet. There *had* to be some way I could help Jax with his PTSD. Even if I was his trigger. The first thing I could do to help him—and us—was to make sure he knew how deeply I was committed to him, no matter what.

I got out of bed and changed into jeans and a t-shirt before checking my phone. It was nine in the morning. People were surely up by now.

But when I went out in the living room, it was empty. I checked every room. Same deal. Somewhat surprised, I decided to head out of the bus and go to the performers area of the festival. It was kind of strange for the entire band to leave the bus so early in the morning, but if they were anywhere then the performers area was probably the place.

As I walked across the festival grounds toward the performers area, my stomach twisted in knots. Why had Jax left me on the tour bus? Why had the entire band left with him? The more I thought about it, the worse I felt. After the talk we'd had last night, being left alone on the tour bus without a word gave me the sinking feeling that Jax was pushing me away.

Sky and Chewie were standing outside and chatting as I approached the performers area. They saw me and waved. I waved back. They got me through security without issue and soon I was talking to Sky face to face while Chewie went to go find Kev.

"Where were you guys this morning?" I asked her, trying to keep my voice casual. "I know I slept in, but it wasn't that late!"

Sky rolled her eyes and jammed her hands in her pockets. "Sorry, Jax had it in his head that we needed to get here early for something, but when we got here it turned out he was wrong."

"Oh," I said, my heart sinking still further. So Jax *had* been the one that got them up and out the door without a thought for me at all. "What did he say it was?"

"Some interview thing," she said with a shrug, her eyes darting around. "After the fire yesterday, I guess. Who knows? Listen, why don't we go get a cup of coffee at the food area? It's still early."

I shook my head. "No, I want to talk to Jax first. Do you know where he is?"

Sky bit her lip. "No. Why don't we get that cup of coffee and you can find him later?"

I pressed my lips together and studied her face. Something was off. "No, I think I'll go to the performer's lounge and wait for him. It's important."

Her face twisted into a brief grimace. "You really don't want to do that. I mean it."

Her words made my mouth feel dry. *What the hell was going on in there?* Waving off Sky's protests, I walked briskly toward the makeshift performers hall, which was usually used for farmers markets. Temporary partitions with flimsy doors separated the individual band areas. After a few minutes, I found the one labelled "Hitchcocks," knocked once, and opened the door.

Jax sat in a chair facing the door. A platinum blonde groupie straddled him. His hands were by his sides. She had her fingers down by his belt buckle and her shirt off, though a black bra was still on.

Anger burned in my chest and made my cheeks flush. The groupie turned with a languid movement when I came in and eyed me curiously.

What was this girl doing with Jax? What was *he* doing with her? My lips curled and I took several shallow breaths. Even though I'd known that Jax and I were on the rocks, I hadn't expected this. I *trusted* him.

But it had happened. Struggling to keep myself steady, I looked this groupie in the eye and pointed to the door. "Get out of here," I said, my voice shaking slightly. "Now."

She turned back to Jax, as if for confirmation. He sighed and pointed to the door himself. "That's my girlfriend," he said tiredly. "You need to go."

She paused for a moment then shrugged, got off of Jax, and retrieved her shirt from the floor. Soon she was gone.

Once the door was closed, I turned to face Jax. He sat and looked at me with his eyes glazed, as if the last bits of his life had been tugged out of him. The sight made me pity him for just a moment before I remembered what I had just seen.

"Jax," I asked quietly, trying to keep myself steady. "What the hell was that?"

He looked away, refusing to meet my eyes, and shook his head.

My jaw clenched. "Who is she?"

He shrugged, refusing to meet my eyes. My heart pounded in my chest as I waited for him to respond, but he wouldn't say a word.

Realization set in. He knew I'd come here. He'd wanted me to catch him. He wanted to push me away.

*But why this way?* I let out a short, dejected sigh as an unbearable weight settled on my chest. "Jax, what are you doing?"

He bit his lip, hard, and after a moment finally looked up at me. "I'm sorry," he said, his voice low as if he didn't have the strength to speak any louder. His dark eyes locked onto mine for a second before he shook his head and let his gaze fall back down to the floor.

I watched him and pressed my lips together, my throat closing tight. "You're sorry?" I choked out. "Is that all you have to say to me right now?"

He froze for several seconds, seemingly gathering himself. "It's done," he said finally, shaking his head. "There's nothing to talk about."

Pain shot through my entire body. I threw my hands up as tears blurred the corners of of my vision. "What's done?" I said through my teeth, struggling to fight back my frustration. "Are you breaking up with me? Because I'm not dumping you just because I caught you pulling some stupid stunt with a groupie."

He flinched, briefly, and rubbed his eyes for several seconds before looking away. I gave him time to get his words together, but after a while he looked back down at the floor.

His silence was killing me. I balled my fists up in frustration. "Damn it, Jax!" I snapped, unable to keep the hurt and bitterness out of my voice, and not caring. "Why are you doing this? Did you ever care about me at all?"

He started, as if snapped out of a trance, and looked up at the ceiling before finally bringing his gaze to meet mine. The shadows under his dark eyes told me he hadn't slept at all, and pain etched deep lines in his face. "Damn it, yes!" he said, his voice tortured. "That's *why* I'm doing this, Riley. Why are you dragging it out and making this worse for both of us?"

Stabbing hurt wracked my body. It was a moment before I could speak, while I weighed each word that I wanted to say to him. "Because I still think we can make it work. Just give us a chance, Jax. You just told me about this yesterday. We haven't had any time to even figure out a way past it."

He shook his head. His unfocused eyes gazed over my shoulder for a moment, then refocused on me. "No. You'll get hurt."

"What, that concert yesterday? Jax, we already—"

"No!" Jax shouted.

I flinched back at his sudden outburst. Finally, he had come to life.

"No," he continued, more quiet but no less intense,"It's not just the concert. It's the fucking nightmares. It's stuff like the shit on the motorcycle. It's me living in terror that I am going to hurt you because of this fucking condition."

I shook my head, not willing to let him make that choice for me. "Jax, I'm not some fragile doll you need to protect. Let me make my own boundaries."

"No," he said firmly, shaking his head. "I can't let you get hurt."

I grimaced and tried to hold myself together. "If you're breaking up with me for my own safety, why can't you let me make that decision?"

He looked back down at the ground. "Because you won't," he said, his voice quiet.

The world seemed to stand still and I swallowed painfully.

He brought his gaze back to meet mine. "You won't leave me, Riley. You'll stick by me until the end. I don't know how it's going to happen, but if we stay together it *will* happen, and it's going to be ugly."

A shiver went down my spine. The hard intensity in his face scared me.

"I can't let that happen," Jax said, his voice nearly a whisper. His dark eyes looked haunted, as if the life had been sucked from him.

I took a deep, shaky breath, trying to calm myself. "If it's really over," I said, my lips trembling despite my attempts to hold it together. "Then say it to my face, Jax. Say you're breaking up with me."

He looked up, squinting, his jaw working slowly. After a deep breath, he looked me right in the eyes, his mouth trembling for a moment before holding firm. "I'm breaking up with you. I'm sorry, Riley. I wish there was another way."

My stomach felt sick as tears rolled messily down my cheeks. This was really happening. After weeks of struggling to figure out what was wrong with Jax, it was over.

I knew Jax was trouble the first time I set eyes on him. What I hadn't counted on was what a sweet, sensitive, romantic man lay beneath that mask. And that I would fall in love with him. Now, the man I fell in love with sat with his shoulders slumped as if he'd been broken. Defeated.

I took a deep, tortured breath and looked at him, my vision blurry with tears. Even if it was over, I needed to make sure he knew I cherished what we'd had. "Well, I still love you," I said shakily, fighting back a sob. "More than anyone I've ever met. Whatever it is you're going through and whatever you do to recover, maybe that will help—that you'll know that I'm out there somewhere, still in love with you."

His head dropped for a moment and he ran his hands through his hair before he looked back up at me. "Riley, I—"

His voice broke, then he was mute, and his head fell lifelessly down. The thought of hugging him one last time crossed my mind, but he hadn't made any movement toward me from his seat, so I didn't. I walked back to the door and turned to say goodbye.

A sob shook me as I opened my mouth to say the word. I couldn't. Tears flowing, I put my hand up lamely to signal I was leaving and stepped out of the room. Then I stormed down the hall quickly and from there away from the performers area to the bus. The vision of him sitting there like a cracked statue haunted me as I left.

We were done. What now?

As I walked, I thought about my friends. Kristen, Jen, even my mom. They were the ones I wanted to talk to. But they were all in New York.

That was where I needed to be.

After stopping by the tour bus to grab my work bag, I called a cab and headed to the nearest main street to be picked up. When the cabbie came, I got in and told him to take me to LAX. I would figure out a flight home to New York when I got there. Then I looked out the window and cried for what Jax and I had lost. I was shattered.

# Chapter Nineteen

## MOVING ON

Manhattan. My island. My home.

I'd been in town for two weeks now, trying to adjust. The skyscraper canyons were a stark contrast to the spacious, palm tree lined California boulevards I'd left behind.

It'd been two weeks without Jax. At first I found myself bursting into tears at random times in the night, my heart hurt so much. But I couldn't go on that way forever. After one too many sleepless nights, I made a plan to get my shit together. I had a life I enjoyed before Jax came into it—I just needed to work on getting back there again.

The first step in getting better was to carefully avoid any websites, magazines, or radio stations where I might see or hear anything about Jax. The less I thought about him, the better.

Despite my precautions, I had a bad moment when a large cardboard box arrived from LA. With my stomach tied up in knots, I'd shoved it in my hall closet, unopened. I guessed that inside Jax had packed all my stuff that I'd left behind on the bus.

I didn't even want to open that box of hurt.

But I'd been through breakups before, and survived. I knew what to do, and that the first few weeks were always the hardest. In a month, I'd forget all about what a fool I'd been over some damn rock star. Hell, I'd probably laugh about it.

Now, though, I would pretend my best that nothing had ever happened between us. And with each day, the hurt would grow less. At least, that was the theory.

Kristen called every couple days, seemingly worried about me. Finally, she wanted me to come over for dinner, but somehow that seemed like too much effort. Just trying to make conversation over the phone had been hard, so I begged off.

I had too much work to do anyway. I'd gotten my twenty thousand dollar bonus for a job well done, but somehow, it seemed like every day I kept falling further and further behind on my assignments. The kudos for my good work as a tour accountant had been short-lived, and just that morning Palmer had chewed me out about a couple of errors on an expense analysis report. It hadn't been pretty.

I sat at my desk, staring at my computer. Numbers swam before my eyes, and I put my head in my hands. If I could just finish up this report, I would go home—and maybe go straight to bed.

The time on my computer said five thirty. I sighed. The day had been hard, but at least I'd managed to get through most of it without thinking about Jax. *See? Progress.*

I heard footsteps behind me, and I hunched over my keyboard, hoping Palmer hadn't caught me slacking.

"Hey, Riley."

I started, and swiveled my head around.

Jen stood there, her purse slung over one shoulder.

"A few of us are going to Mickey's Pub. Want to come?"

I exhaled slowly, trying to soothe my frayed nerves. "Nah. I'm just going to finish up here and go home."

Jen frowned. "When you took a pass on happy hour last Friday, I thought, gee, she must be tired from her trip. But two weeks in a row? That's unheard of."

I looked up at her and then glanced away, fighting down a growing uneasiness. I hadn't lied to Jen about what had happened between me and Jax—but I hadn't told her the whole truth either. The thought of hearing her say "I told you so" was absolutely the last humiliation I wanted to face, so I'd smoothed out the details some, leaving out the heartbreak and passing the whole affair off as some crazy, short-lived fling.

Jen grabbed a chair from the cubicle next to mine and sat down in it. Rolling a little closer, she leaned forward with a suspicious look on her face. "I mean, this is ironic. Here I am, begging you to go out with me. Usually it's the other way around."

I shrugged and gave her a weak smile that felt all wrong on my face. "Maybe I'm just finally getting my priorities straight. There's more to life than just the weekend."

Jen whistled. "Words I never thought I'd hear. I don't think you mean it."

My face grew hot. "Well, I do. If there's one thing I learned from being out on the road, it's that I don't want to live on the edge. Not anymore."

Her eyes widened. "Who are you, and what have you done with my friend Riley? Living on the edge is your MO."

"The longer you stay on the edge," I replied, unable to keep the bitterness out of my voice, "The more likely you are to get hurt."

"I don't know what happened to you out there," Jen said, her face solemn, "But it sounds like you got hurt already."

My heart wrenched, and I struggled to keep my face composed. From her serious face, I could tell I no longer had her fooled. But I was getting better now. I should be able to talk about it, no big deal.

I sighed deeply and shook my head. "You were right. About Jax. But it's nothing I can't handle."

Jen gave me a penetrating look. "I'm not going to stand around telling you 'I told you so.' I think you're doing a good enough job of that on your own."

My face flushed red. She seemed to know exactly the reason why I had kept my time with Jax so secret. "It was too embarrassing to talk about at first. But I'm doing okay now, so what the hell."

She leaned forward. "But honey, *are* you handling it okay? All the concealer in the world can't hide those dark circles under your eyes. Your butt has been parked in that chair all day, so I know you didn't go get lunch." Her eyes suddenly grew worried. "Have you even eaten at all today?"

I jutted out my chin and glared at her. "Cereal this morning."

"That's it?" Jen exclaimed. "Look, I know the symptoms of a broken heart. And you've got all of them."

I frowned, but her words cut me to the core. My heart might have *been* broken, but couldn't she see I was moving on? I exhaled a shaky breath. "No I don't. I'm way better off without him. Actually, I'm glad we broke up, because my life is complicated enough without all his drama."

Jen gave me a critical look and stood up. "Uh huh. Right. There's only one remedy for heartbreak. Let's ditch the other girls and you and I will go get dinner. You can talk all you want. Or not. Whatever you want to do is fine. But it's never good to just sit and stew over some asshole who doesn't appreciate a good thing when he sees it."

Her words sent an unexpected shiver of hurt down my spine. *Jax appreciates me. It's just too hard for him to fight for me.*

"It's not like that," I protested. "He cares about me." A lump rose in my throat. "And I care about him too."

"Then why did you break up?" Jen asked, her voice soft.

Tears formed in the corner of my eyes. "I don't know. Our lives are too different. Like I said, I'm better off."

Jen reached out and squeezed my shoulder. "Love isn't something you can talk yourself out of. If you feel that way, and he does too, maybe there's a way you can make it work after all."

I shook my head as a tear coursed down my cheek. I had wanted to make it work, but nothing would ever have been enough to stop Jax's pain from tearing us apart. "I tried. I can't try anymore."

Glancing at her watch, Jen stood up. "Come on, I think you need a drink."

"It's really not that bad," I said, wishing we'd never started this conversation. I'd been doing so well—or so I'd thought. "Thanks for the offer, but I should stay here." I wiped my eyes and gestured towards my computer. "I should finish this. Rain check?"

Jen's brow furrowed, but then she gave me a reluctant smile. "I'm holding you to that. Next week?"

"Sure," I said, turning back to my computer screen and pretending to be lost in a column of numbers. "Have a good weekend."

"You too." Jen's footsteps padded away as she left my cubicle.

The minute she was gone, I closed my eyes and leaned back in my chair. My head throbbed.

Maybe Jen was right, and I should eat. Getting up, I headed into the break room to go forage for food in the breakroom. Maybe someone left a ramen packet in there for poor fools like me who had to work late.

I opened a cupboard, and my tired eyes scanned the contents. A stack of packaged ramen noodles stood in the corner, looking forlorn. *Oh joy.*

As I waited for the microwave to cook my unappetizing dinner, I sat down at the table. In the center stood two shakers, one salt, and one pepper.

*Pepper. His stupid nickname for me.*

My breath caught in my throat. I reached for the shaker and closed my eyes tight. *It's like he's everywhere.*

The ache in my heart suddenly hurt as fresh as the moment Jax wounded it. I tried to block the fleeting images, but they appeared in front of my eyes like they'd been burned into me permanently: Jax's rough hands caressing my body. His intense look of lust as he saw me naked for the first time. His hair, twisted around my fingers on the pillow in the morning sun.

A deep longing settled like a weight on my chest. Jax had been mine. I'd loved him, and having him for such a short time only made the hurt feel worse.

I curled my hand into a tight fist around the pepper shaker, digging my nails into the soft skin of my palms. But feeling this way wasn't something I could keep on doing. The truth was, Jax's problems had turned out to be more than our love for each other could handle.

I had to face the reality: I wasn't like Kristen. There was no perfect love waiting to sweep me off my feet, and believing there was had come close to costing me my job—or my life.

So I'd put my nose to the grindstone, get my work done. I'd find someone new. Somebody compatible and reasonable and perfectly suitable, not just someone who made my heart beat faster every time I saw him.

I took one last look at the pepper shaker before flinging it at the wall with enough force to make it bounce off the tile floor as I turned to leave the kitchen.

I'd never love anyone as much as I'd loved Jax.

But maybe it was better that way.

# Chapter Twenty

## FUCK

**Jax**

I slowly opened my eyes, then stared at the unfamiliar ceiling and closed them again with a sigh. This wasn't my bedroom.

After opening them again, I groaned and rolled myself to a seated position. Leather creaked beneath me as I moved. Couch. The couch on the bus. Not too bad. I must have passed out after a night out drinking.

As I took stock of my surroundings, I saw a nearly empty whiskey bottle sitting on the coffee table, practically taunting me.

So *that* was why I was feeling like such shit. My head spun. That was about right.

It had been two weeks in hell after Riley had left. The nightmares were gone, along with all the other shit that had been plaguing me from the PTSD. The doc had been right about Riley. She'd been the trigger.

But having her gone wasn't helping my music. The band was in the middle of a recording session, and every song I wrote sucked. I knew it. But there was nothing I could do.

Riley's face haunted me wherever I went, no matter what I was doing. So after our recording session inevitably broke up with everyone pissed off, I drank. Tried to forget. And failed, every damn time.

I rubbed my hands over my face, then grabbed the whiskey bottle off the table. *If this doesn't kill me, her memory will anyway.* Grimacing, I opened the bottle, craned my neck back, and took a slug. As I wiped my mouth with the back of my hand, footsteps sounded on the stairs.

Sky emerged from her bedroom and came into the common area where I sat. Her eyes locked on mine. I set the whiskey bottle down, and she frowned.

"You look like you got hit by a truck," she said, dropping down on the couch next to me. Her eyes seemed serious as she studied my face.

I shrugged, avoiding her gaze. "Well, it's nothing you haven't seen before."

She exhaled. "No, this is different," she said. Leaning forward, she peered at me with an intense expression on her face. "*You're* different."

I drew my brows together. I didn't like where this was going. "Just need a little more hair of the dog," I replied, unable to keep the irritation out of my voice. "Then I'll be fine."

"No, Jax, you're not fine," she said, then hesitated for a moment, biting her lip. "I've been wanting to talk to you about it."

I groaned. "Can we have your episode of Intervention sometime when I'm not hungover?"

Her eyes were big and sad. "When do you think that'll be? When you're dead?"

Closing my eyes, I pressed a hand to my throbbing head. "I'll stop drinking when I don't need it any more. Promise."

"Do you need it because of Riley?" she asked, her voice soft, but persistent.

*Fuck.* My heart throbbed. I lay back down on the couch.

Sky continued, her voice gaining strength as she went on. "I'm not blind, Jax."

I exhaled. Sky sat on the couch with her arms folded, waiting for my answer. There was no avoiding her, and in my hungover state, it was too hard to even try.

"I haven't been myself lately," I said slowly. "I didn't want to hurt her any more than I already have."

"Did she tell you she's been hurt?" Sky asked.

"No, but I've hurt her already, and we can't be together or I'm going to hurt her more."

She exhaled with frustration. "Jax, what's this really about?"

I gave her an icy look. "It's none of your business."

She waited for more, and when nothing was forthcoming she sighed again. "Listen, I know things have been messed up with you for a while, but I thought Riley changed that for you. Am I wrong? Weren't things better with her?"

Her words shot a bolt of pain in my gut. "I don't have a choice, Sky!" I snapped, unable to keep the bitterness out of my voice. "Just leave it alone. Leave me alone."

"And what?" she spat back at me. "Watch until you drink yourself into a coma because you won't let anyone care about you?"

I flinched and searched for a comeback. I didn't want to tell her about everything that had happened with my dad, so there wasn't anything to say.

She sighed, and her face looked more frustrated than I'd ever seen it. "Jax, you don't have to tell me what's going on. But the way you're acting, I think you need to talk to her. You need to do *something*."

I shook my head. "I'll handle a breakup however I want."

"Oh, look at the tough guy!" Sky cried, her eyes narrowing skeptically.

"What do you want, me to cry on your shoulder?" I said with a sneer.

She gave me a scornful look. "Fine, if you want to be tough, whatever. But think about how she feels. She knows that you love her, and she loves you, but you won't be in a relationship with her. That has to be breaking her heart."

Her words sent a shiver through my body, taking the fight out of me. "Even if that were true," I said, my voice low, "It doesn't make any difference now. I fucked everything up, big time."

"It's not too late. If you love her, you need to tell her."

I jutted out my chin. "But what if I hurt her even more by trying to come back now? Maybe she'd be better off if I stayed lost."

She shrugged. "I don't know. She might think that. I tried calling her a few times just to see how she was, and she never answered. But maybe she'll answer for you." She patted my shoulder. "All you can do is try."

"Maybe," I said, my eyes downcast.

Sky stood up. "Jax, I know you have baggage," she said with a compassionate look on her face. "Don't let it ruin your life. Or Riley's."

She left the living room. I heard her moving around in the kitchen, but the noises seemed far away to me. I lay on the couch, staring at the ceiling, lost in thought.

What if she was right? Could Riley and I have a future together? All I wanted to do was protect her from getting hurt—but I already might have hurt her more by pushing her away.

Sighing, I got up and grabbed my jacket from off the floor where I must have tossed it last night. As my hand closed around it, a crunching sound came from one of the inside pockets.

I reached my hand in curiously. My fingers touched paper, and I pulled it out. I stared down at what I held with surprise.

It was an envelope. With words written on it: *For when the shows are over.*

*Riley.* This was her gift to me. Not to be opened until we were apart. Somehow I'd forgotten all about it.

My fingers trembled as they smoothed the slightly crumpled envelope. With one smooth tug, I ripped it open. Out came an SD card like the kind I recorded music on, and a piece of paper. I scanned the letter with eager eyes.

But it wasn't a letter. It was lyrics.

*How can I write you something new*
*when everything's been said?*
*How do I tell you all the sweet things*
*I'm feeling in my head?*

*Three little chords is all it takes*
*to write a song that sounds new*
*And three little words is all I need*
*To tell you that I love you.*

*So if you're feeling lonely*

*And if you're feeling blue*
*play these three chords and I'll remember*
*that you love me, too.*

My heart tightened, and I closed my eyes. *Riley.*

# Chapter Twenty-One

## IT'S A BOY

**Riley**

Squinting at Kristen's bulging belly, I gathered a long piece of string.

Immediately, she burst into howls of laughter. "Riley," she gasped between laughs. "I know I'm huge but there's *no way* I'm that big!"

The other women at the baby shower giggled, and I sheepishly cut the string. Kristen looped the big ball of string around herself, snipped it off when it was all the way around her belly, and then spooled it away from herself and compared it to the strings held out by all the other women at the party. "The closest guess, and the prize, goes to . . . Lauren!"

Lauren got up to get her gift basket, already starting to waddle from her own pregnancy. I glanced, for what must have been the fiftieth time, at the clock in my living room. How much longer was this going to go on?

When her venue cancelled, having Kristen's baby shower in my apartment had seemed like a good idea—at first. After all, a party planner was taking care of the details, which meant I mostly had to stand around as the caterers and decorators came by. Supervising the setup was at least something to do that wasn't binge-watching entire seasons of America's Next Top Model or scarfing down a tub of Cherry Garcia.

My feelings changed, though, when the first guests started to arrive.

Most of them, I didn't know at all—they were the wives of Vincent's friends, incredibly wealthy women whose clothes probably cost more than I made in a month. As they started to make small talk about their fabulous lives, their fabulous marriages, and their even more fabulous pregnancies, I started to feel myself go numb.

This was foreign territory to me. I'd never even lived with a boyfriend, and with Jax's breakup still fresh on my mind, I couldn't help but feel intimidated and a little— scratch that, a *lot*—left out by the whole thing.

So I'd spent my time talking to caterers, hanging back in the corners, and finding ways to mentally block the baby vibes. It wasn't a perfect solution, but Kristen seemed to think I was just especially dedicated to making sure the logistics of the party were sorted.

Every time I looked at her, radiant with baby glow, I felt a twinge of envy through my congratulatory smiles. I knew we weren't in a competition, but I couldn't help feeling like she'd won a lottery that I hadn't even been able to keep a ticket for.

"Listen up, everyone!" Kristen said, breaking me out of my thoughts. "Next we're decorating onesies! Everyone has a blank white one and some markers underneath their chair. When the baby's born, we'll be using these, so let's see some creativity!"

She shot me a grin, and I smiled weakly back. "Hey, Riles, get over here," she said, opening her arms as if to hug me. "Bring your onesie, too. We'll do this one together."

I walked over to her couch and gave her a big hug. A look of concern passed over her face. "You okay? I worried this might not be a good idea so soon after Ja—"

"What did we agree about that name?" I asked, arching an eyebrow.

She made a zipping motion over her lips. "Right. He Whose Name Shall Not Be Spoken. Anyway, if you need to get out of here, I understand. The estrogen level in this room is way beyond the sanity point."

I shook my head, sitting on the couch next to her. "This is a huge day for you. I'm not going to let some stupid washed-up rock star ruin it for either of us."

"Good," she said, reaching for a yellow marker in a coffee table basket. "The shower's almost over anyway. Just a few marked-up onesies and party favors to go."

I smiled at her, grabbing a green marker. "Thanks, Kristen."

"For what?"

"Telling me we should have the baby shower here," I said. "I know I've complained about it, but at least it gave me something to do."

"Why do you think I asked you to do it here?" she said, a mischievous twinkle in her eye as she drew a yellow sun.

"You told me the venue cancelled."

"Because you'd have never done it otherwise. But look, it helped, didn't it?"

I nodded, smiling. It was just like her to tell the white lie for my benefit, and she was right: keeping busy had helped. Helping get the shower ready, at least, had been good for me.

So why was it that as soon as I was in the party itself, my enthusiasm was gone?

"I don't know what's wrong with me, Kris," I admitted, drawing what I hoped looked like a turtle on the onesie. "I know Jax and me would never work, it's just—I look at all this, and I feel like everyone here is with their special person. And for a little while, I really thought I'd found mine."

She looked into my eyes with concern. "It's okay to have a broken heart, you know," she said. "And it's okay you didn't take anyone's advice. I like that you don't do what everyone says. It gives you the best stories."

That brought a small smile to my face. "Thanks, Kris. I needed that." I added a face to the turtle with a red marker.

A breeze wafted through the curtains, and I heard an acoustic guitar strum on the street below. *A C chord*, I realized, the bittersweet memory of playing among the broken guitars flashing into my head. *Jax taught me that.* I tried to shut the memory out.

Then a D chord played. And a G. *Just three chords, and you can play a song . . .*

I shook my head. This was no time to get all nostalgic. "That window *cannot* stay open," I said, rising from the couch.

The three chords played in succession as I walked toward the billowing curtains. C, D, G. C, D, G.

*Pssssssh. Anyone can do that. Even I can do that.*

And then I heard a deep voice:

*How can I write you something new*
*when everything's been said?*

*How do I tell you all the sweet things*
*I'm feeling in my head?*

*My song.* My silly lyrics I'd written after Jax taught me how to play guitar. What the hell was going on? Was this some kind of sick joke? I flung the curtains to the side and looked out the window.

There, on the sidewalk, I saw Jax strumming an acoustic guitar, singing the song I'd written him. Jax, in the flesh, his body skimmed by the same black t-shirt and blue jeans he wore during the tour, his hair falling untamed around his eyes. He was still the most gorgeous man I had ever seen.

I watched him, and suddenly it felt like someone had punched me in the gut.

Because it didn't change anything. He'd ended things childishly, pushed me away as hard as he could. He'd told me I was the trigger to his trauma.

So why was he underneath my window, singing the lyrics of the song I'd written him?

As I stuck my head out the window, he looked up at me, and our eyes met, his scarred brow rising. *Is this really happening?*

And then, the last stanza of my song ended, but he was still singing—words I hadn't written, lyrics I'd never heard before, with a new chord added seamlessly to the structure, one I didn't know how to play:

*You meant more than I could know*
*When I forced you to leave*
*Since the day I watched you go*

*I can barely breathe*

*You may wonder whether*
*what we had was true*
*But I break when we're not together*
*I'm myself when I'm with you*

Behind me, the entire baby shower was watching me at the window. The women started talking excitedly behind their hands as the verse ended.

"Jax," I breathed as my jaw slackened, unable to fully comprehend what was happening. He'd caused me so much pain, but now he was right here, asking for . . . what? Forgiveness? A second chance? He was incredibly gorgeous, but his face was almost painful for me to look at after everything that he'd said the last time we'd been together.

He played a final chord, then looked up with soulful eyes. "Riley, let me come up. Please. I just want to talk."

I tore my eyes away, suddenly paralyzed with indecision. He'd made a sweet gesture—but he'd also made a complete disaster of things when we were together. Eyes wide, I turned around to Kristen. "Oh God, Kris, what do I do?"

One of the baby shower attendees, a woman I'd only met a few times named Bev, butted in with a response before Kristen could say anything. "Is he serenading you? That's so freaking romantic," she said, her voice sounding dreamy.

Kristen narrowed her eyes. "That's Riley's ex," she said, and Bev suddenly bit her lip, looking chastised.

"And I was hoping I'd never have to see him again," I said to Kristen. "So of course he shows up."

Kristen eyed me with one brow raised. "Hey, I'm all for girl power, but are you sure that's what you really think? To me, it sure looks like you've been pining over him since you left California."

I glared at her. "You're *not* helping." The last thing I needed was a reminder of how emotionally bereft Jax's breakup had left me.

"Suit yourself," she said, stirring her virgin cocktail idly. "I'd just hate for you to regret later on that you didn't talk to him. Even if it's just to tell him to fuck off."

Bev gave me a look with one raised eyebrow. "He's got a pretty great voice. And he's *gorgeous*. If you don't want him, I'll take him."

We both shot her a dismayed glance, and she was quiet again.

"Look," I said, a skeptical look on my face, "I'm not going to set myself up to get hurt again. After how we ended, why would I even want to listen to what he has to say?"

"You don't have to jump into bed with him," Kristen said. "I'm just saying, hear the guy out. Let him speak his piece. He obviously cares a lot, or he wouldn't be here."

"So, what, you're saying I should just invite him up? *Now?* In the middle of your baby shower with half the socialites in Manhattan attending? If he wants to come up that badly, he can wait for a better time."

Suddenly, Kristen got a mischievous look in her eye.

"Ladies!" she yelled, tapping a spoon to her glass to get the room's attention. "This party is officially moving down the block to the first cafe we find, whether Riley likes it or not, and I don't want to hear any complaints. Got it?"

The women immediately erupted into chatter, and Kristen leaned out the window. "Riley wants to see you up here. Third floor." She paused, looking around the room at the mess we'd made for the party, then seemed to consider. "Maybe you'd better give her ten minutes."

My eyes flickered instantly to the clock: 2:07. Giggles and murmurs came up from the crowd as everyone started to move toward the door at once—even the caterers. My jaw gaped open as I looked at Kristen. "Why are you doing this for me?" I asked. "You don't even want me to be with Jax."

She shook her head and took both my hands into hers. "I want you to be happy, Riley. And I know you've been really unhappy for weeks. If that man down there makes you feel better . . ." she said, tilting her head toward the window, "then I'm not going to stand in the way. Hear him out, tell him to go to hell if you need to, and call me if you need anything at all."

My eyes filled with tears. Her friendship meant more to me than I could ever say. "Thanks, Kris," I whispered.

"It's nothing. Now wipe those tears away before he comes up here!" She grabbed her purse and made a beeline for the door.

Dabbing my eyes as I moved through my living room, I looked around. *There's no way you can cover this mess up*, I realized, looking around as the last guest closed the door behind her.

In a frenzy, I shoved piles of baby presents and marked-up onesies toward one corner before snatching down banners and stuffing them into the pile. I crammed plates into the sink and stopped for a moment to look at myself in the full-length hallway mirror. *Shit.* My hair was kind of a mess, my dress was rumpled from sitting. The clock read 2:14. Only seven minutes had passed.

And then I heard a knock.

# Chapter Twenty-Two

### FEARLESS

I walked toward the door, my heart thumping practically out of my chest. Before I could even reach the knob, the door opened inward, revealing Jax, in the flesh, suddenly so close I could catch a hint of his scent.

"I couldn't wait ten minutes," he said, his low voice sending tremors through my body. The raw earthiness of him reminded me of the passionate embraces we'd once shared, and a stab of pain shivered through my body. To see him again, and to know I had lost him, tore my heart in two.

"Jax!" I said, my voice sharp with hurt. "What are you doing here?"

He slung the guitar off his shoulder and rested it on the floor. Without it he suddenly seemed at a loss for words. He took a deep breath and looked me in the eyes before he began to speak. "I had to see you. I didn't know if you'd let me come up, but I had to talk to you."

"Well . . . you're here now," I said dubiously. My heart ached with longing, but I wasn't about to show him any vulnerability. I couldn't—not after what happened last time. It was already too much. "I kind of thought you'd said everything you needed to say."

He flinched. "I did a lot of stupid things when we were together," he said quietly. There was pain behind his eyes as he looked at me, but he didn't break away. "I'm sorry. I know I fucked up. The things I'm about to tell you don't come easy. So I'm going to need you to just listen for a minute. Okay?"

I pressed my lips closed tight, a renewed frustration coiling up in my chest. After the way Jax and I had ended, I wasn't sure what he had left to say. Questions flooded my mind. Didn't it make him crazy when he saw me? Would he hallucinate, or freeze up? Why come here and take the risk?

I gave him a curt nod and stepped aside. He walked slowly into my apartment and stopped, as if not sure if he was welcome any further. Standing there, he took a deep breath and closed his eyes. When he opened them again, he started to speak in a low, strained voice.

"I know this is selfish but I *need* you. Every day without you is like trying to breathe underwater. I'm drowning, Riley. I know I said it was impossible for us to be together, but . . . I want to give us a chance. Tell me we can make this work."

I stood there, reeling. I'd never expected so much emotion to come at once from Jax. It was a good speech. For some girls, maybe it would have been enough. But not me. I couldn't let him back into my heart, because I couldn't stop thinking about how hard he'd pushed me away.

So I pushed back. "You know, that's what I was about to do, that day at the festival. I was about to tell you we could make it work. And instead of talking to me, you tried to push me away with some silicon-enhanced bimbo."

"I deserve that," he said quietly, looking stung. "I know that was crazy."

"And stupid. And childish."

He nodded, looking ashamed. "I'm sorry, Riley. My mind was racing. All I could think about was what my therapist had said. I felt like a ticking time bomb. I needed something that would make you leave right away. All I wanted was for you to be far enough from me that you weren't caught up in the blast."

I licked my lips, the bitter taste of the memory washing over me as fresh as the day it happened. "Because when I'm around you, you feel worse," I said. "At least, that's what you said then. What's so different now?"

"What's different is that now I'm sure I won't direct those feelings at you. I'm going to work through them and make sure they never hurt you again."

"It's not that easy, Jax," I said, folding my arms in front of my chest. "If we got back together, wouldn't I just keep reminding you of Darrel?"

His nostrils flared, and his chiseled features grew hard. "Of all the things I hate that prick for, the biggest one is that I drove you away because of him. I'm done with having my life controlled by a sick, twisted old man."

My heart leapt at the fire and conviction in his voice, but I couldn't help worrying that he was promising more than he could deliver. "So what, you're all better now?" I asked, desperately trying to keep the skepticism in my voice. "Done with the breaking things, the hallucinations? Just like that?"

He took my chin into his hand, cradling it as he looked into my eyes. Against my will, my heart felt warmed by his touch. "I'm saying that from now on, I'm not taking that pain and anger out on the band, or on you. Darrel hurt me, but I can't let him win. I can't let him control my life forever. I can't let his anger keep hurting us both."

I looked at him closely, surprised at how his words resonated with what I'd been thinking the night before we broke up. It wasn't like him to talk so much about emotions, or Darrel. "Are you still going to therapy?"

"I am," he said, the words spilling out quickly. "And will be for a long time. It doesn't get better overnight. I'm just getting better at directing my anger in therapy, not at everyone around me."

I swallowed. Did I trust Jax enough to give him another chance? Kristen was right, my heart yearned to take him back—I'd been fighting my longing for him for weeks. But my mind knew there were still a hundred things that could go wrong. "It's a big risk," I said quietly. "For you as much as for me."

"It's a risk. But it's a bigger risk to lose you. You're my inspiration. You're all I think about. I . . ." he paused, seemingly steeling himself. "I love you, Riley."

Time stopped. Suddenly, I felt like I could hear every noise in the room: the blades of the ceiling fan circling through the air. The street vendors three stories below taking orders. My own beating heart.

In all the time I'd known Jax, that was a word I'd never heard pass his lips. Not even when I'd said it to him.

It was the biggest little word that had ever come between us. I stood there, speechless.

"I love you," he said, reaching for my cheek. "I don't know how long I've loved you, but I know that when you're gone, it's like the music goes out of my bones. I acted like a complete idiot to make you leave, and I refuse to make the same mistake twice. I love you."

I squeezed his hand instinctively even as what-ifs swirled around in my mind. While I was sure Jax would get better than he'd been at the end of the tour, there was no guarantee he'd ever fully recover from his trauma. But he was taking responsibility, admitting he was wrong . . . and showing that he was going to make it different this time around.

But it was more than that, I knew, feeling warmth suffuse through me. I'd never felt as at home with anyone. I'd never known someone who could make my heart beat faster like he did, just from being in the same room. I'd never known anyone who made me laugh so hard.

I searched for words, trying to figure out how to tell him what I was feeling. "I've been wanting to hear that for a while," I said slowly.

"I know. And I understand if you can't take me back, or won't. I fucked things up. I did things I can't take back."

He looked miserable, but I wasn't finished yet. "I've been thinking about love a lot since you made me leave," I said, keeping my voice even, though my heart was pounding wildly. "Because falling in love with you was easy. Too easy."

"Easy doesn't begin to describe it," Jax admitted. "I don't think I could have helped it if I'd tried."

"But people say love is hard work for a reason. It's hard work because it means you have to choose to keep it up, even when things are hard."

"I know. And I let you down." His face twisted with disappointment.

I shook my head and looked up at him. "That kind of trying takes two people. If I'm going to do this again, I can't be the only one who's willing to keep going when things are hard."

"You won't be." His hand reached out toward my face, but instead brushed against the "It's a Boy" banner hanging on the cabinet next to me.

Suddenly, he paused with a quizzical look, seeming to notice the apartment for the first time, and let go of my arms. His brow furrowed as he took in the disaster area of the baby shower's aftermath. He gently lifted a corner of the banner, blinking incredulously. "Is this . . . Riley, are you having a baby?"

We'd always used protection, and anyhow, even if somehow I'd gotten pregnant with Jax, it would have been way too early for me to have had a baby shower. Then again, as a rock star, I doubted Jax had been to many baby showers. I couldn't resist a moment of teasing.

"So what if I am?" I said, flicking one eyebrow up.

His face contorted, expressions flickering across his eyes that I couldn't understand. "Oh my God, Riley. I'm so sorry you didn't feel like you could tell me . . ." He took a deep breath. "It's going to be okay. If we can get through that night at Darrel's, we can get through this, too. Together."

I burst out into a laugh. "Jax! I wasn't serious!"

He squinted at me, looking utterly baffled. I'd only meant to tease him a little. Instead, he was telling me that he was willing to try parenting with me—I couldn't help but feel secretly a little bit happy, even though the rational side of me said *one step at a time.*

"There's no baby," I said. "Well, there *is* a baby. But it's not mine. This party was for my best friend, Kristen."

Relief flooded his face, and his arms enclosed around me again.

"Riley, I want to make this work, whatever it takes. You're my inspiration," he said, caressing the small of my back. "Your song brought me back from the brink. Until I heard it, it was like I couldn't write anything. I couldn't sing anything."

I blushed. "It wasn't much of a song."

"It was *yours*. And that's all that mattered." His eyes shone into me like a fire, warming me from the inside out. "You're worth holding onto, whatever it takes. I'm never going to push you away again. Just . . . tell me you'll let me try to make this work."

His words struck me to my core, and my soul thrilled with the conviction that he'd meant every one of them. "If we're going to do this, it's going to take both of us," I said, my heart beating wildly. "It's going to be a lot of hard work."

His hard features suddenly seemed softer, more hopeful. "Are you saying you still want to try?"

"I'm saying that I love you, Jax." I wrapped my arms around him. "And if we love each other, then there's only one way we can do it."

His scarred brow raised, a silent question mark.

"Fearlessly," I said, standing on tiptoes to touch my lips to his.

In an instant, I felt his mouth pressing against mine as he pinned me back against the wall. My lips parted, and I felt his tongue slide in, sensuous and warm, sending a thrill into me that went all the way to my fingertips.

My head spun with desire as we clutched each other close. He moved his lips away, then brought them back to mine for another kiss, even more passionate than the last.

My fingers moved to the hem of his t-shirt, lifting it up over his taut muscles, and I stared with naked, unabashed lust at the golden skin of his chest. Before I could say anything more, his hands had started to strip my clothes away, and I felt my bra unhooking behind me as my top came off. Strong hands lifted me upward, and my legs wrapped instinctively around Jax's waist. Devouring one another's mouths hungrily, we shed pieces of clothing one at a time.

When we got to my bed, he laid me down in it gently, staring down at me with a tenderness I'd never seen in him before. But there was something else, too, something new and possessive and primal. I couldn't wait to see where our bodies would take us next.

"I love you, Jax," I said, quivering with anticipation as he stood naked at the bed's edge, lit by the afternoon sun.

He teased my legs apart with gentle hands. "I love you, too, Riley," he said, kissing the inside of my thighs.

We didn't get out of bed until the next morning.

# Epilogue

*Five months later*

The steam shower felt almost too good to get out of, but the evening was barely getting started.

I turned the faucet off, casting a regretful look at the bathroom. *Too bad we're only staying until Monday*, I thought. There were a lot of things New York City did better than Hollywood, but hotel suite bathrooms were definitely not among them.

As I toweled off my wet hair, I looked down at the bathroom counter. The L.A. Times was folded over to a headline: *Arsonist Gets Third Strike*. I touched the newspaper with damp fingers, feeling victorious as I read the lines. Thanks to a couple of previous felony charges for grand theft auto, it looked like Darrel was never going to be seeing the outside of a prison cell again.

And it was all because of us.

When the arson investigators called a few weeks after Jax and I got back together, they wanted to talk about Anarchy Fest. Apparently, they'd found evidence of arson but most of their leads had gone cold, so they were asking performers.

We told them everything we knew—and I even remembered to tell the investigators that Jax thought he'd seen Darrel. It turned out the side of the stage where Jax spotted him was right where the fire had started. They took it as a tip and searched his property, and found plenty of evidence for not just the Anarchy Fest arson, but half a dozen other unsolved crimes related to the Reapers.

They even found pictures he'd taken of us, showing how he'd followed Jax and me almost everywhere after that night. After Jax realized his "hallucinations" had actually been Darrel, he calmed down a lot. Every week, he was making progress in therapy, and his nightmares were getting under control.

I smiled, taking one last look at the article, and tossed the paper in the trash. Sometimes, you really could put the past behind you.

On the counter below the paper was a tiny box, with a little note on top. "With so much to celebrate, I couldn't resist. — J"

I grinned at the surprise—he must have left it there while I was showering. Opening the lid, I saw a dangling pair of earrings that dripped with emeralds and diamonds. *Oh my god, Jax.* I marveled as I took them out of their velvet-lined box, watching how the gems sparkled in the light. They matched my dress for the show perfectly.

Suddenly, I had an idea. I twisted my hair up, put the earrings on one by one, then dropped the towel.

The earrings glittered enticingly, contrasting against my pale skin and red hair. *Perfect.* I walked out of the bathroom wearing nothing but a seductive smile.

"I know you probably got them to match my dress," I said, turning the corner to the suite bedroom. Jax, his back turned to me, stood half-dressed next to the bedroom's sunken tub. "I thought you might like them better like this."

He turned around to face me, and his brow rose in a sexy arch as a broad smile spread across his lips. "You were right," he said, taking off the pants he'd clearly just put on. God, I loved the sight of his naked body—I never got tired of watching him strip. "I like it so much, in fact, that it makes me remember a certain night in Las Vegas."

On the nightstand, a ringtone started playing from Jax's phone. I looked toward it, and then toward him. "That was a good night," I said, ignoring the phone to wrap my arms around his bare skin. It had been ringing off the hook with interview requests ever since news broke about the nomination—and the last thing either of us wanted right at this moment was media attention.

Jax brought his mouth down to hover near my ear, sending a shiver through my shower-damp body. "I'm aching for you, Riley."

I looked down to see his erection, thick and rock-hard, and felt warm wetness starting to develop between my legs. He brought a finger slowly down my chest and stomach, then further down until I gasped with pleasure.

He teased at the wet folds gently, slowly, until I felt like my body was on fire with yearning for his touch. His lips brushed against my ear as he said:

"Wrap your legs around me. I want you. Now."

Distantly, I registered another ringtone playing, but I had more important things to do. I brought my legs up around his strong, muscular thighs, longing to feel him inside me. Looking into my eyes, he stepped into the sunken tub, carrying me with seemingly effortless ease.

With the warm water all around us, I brought my hand up to his face, tucking a tendril of his long hair back behind his ear—and then I felt him slip into me, filling me deeply, all at once, making my back arch with surprise and pleasure.

I loved how he fit inside me, and I gasped as he thrust in rhythm. His hands grasped my hips as we moved as one, bringing each other close to the edge of ecstasy.

Using tight, controlled thrusts, he skillfully found my rhythms, going deeper just when I needed it, just when my eyes pleaded for more. I'd never had a lover like Jax—one whose skills just kept getting better the longer we stayed together.

As his body pressed in close against mine, his cock ramming into me harder, faster, I found myself getting closer and closer to the point of no return. The ringtone kept blaring, but I just didn't care. His eyes looked into me, as if they could see all the way through me, intense, always watching, always aware of my pleasure.

My climax began with an intensity that shocked even me, bubbling through my body like orgasmic champagne, rising from the tips of my toes to the top of my head. I screamed out, thrashing in the water as my body clenched down around him, and saw his eyes grow wide with sensation as his orgasm rocked his body.

As the wave of pleasure receded, we looked at each other. "Good timing," I said.

"I try," he said, giving my ass a playful smack, and we both started laughing.

Suddenly, we heard the telltale sound of a card key being inserted into the hotel room lock. Both of us covered our bodies instinctively as the door sprung open with the sound of loud chatter.

"We tried calling," Kev's voice called out above the din, "but you guys didn't—"

When Kev turned the corner to the bedroom, Jax was standing in the sunken tub, struggling to get himself covered, and I was hiding behind him, my elbows and face poking out from behind his body.

"I think maybe you'd better wait out in the hall," Jax said gruffly, his face remaining totally expressionless while Kev's went beet red.

"I think you're right, buddy," Kev said, shielding his eyes. "You guys take your time. But, uh, not too much. I'm pretty sure they don't stop the Grammys for anybody. Not even the favorites."

\*\*\*

An hour and a half later, as I sat sipping champagne from back seat of a limo, Sky pointed excitedly at a crowd gathering on a sidewalk ahead. "We're almost there! Look!"

In front of the crowd, a huge vintage limo stopped, and we watched a couple in formal clothes get out while being swarmed by fans. "Is that Brangelina?" I whispered to Sky, who nodded wordlessly, mouth agape.

We slowed to a crawl in the line of limos letting people out. When it was finally our turn, Jax turned to me. "You ready?" he asked.

"Ready as I'll ever be," I said, taking one last look in my compact mirror before putting it back in my bag.

The driver opened the limo door, and the band stepped out onto the red carpet, dates in tow. Jax and I stepped out last, and were nearly blinded by the flood of flashbulbs that surrounded us.

Reporters and audience members screamed a hundred questions at once as we stepped down the long red carpeted hallway. It took half an hour to walk fifty feet while interviewers shoved mics in the band's faces and stopped them for press photos.

"Is it true that all the songs on your album were written in just two weeks' time?"

"That's right," he said, flashing a grin and squeezing me close to him as he answered the question. "But then, I had some pretty amazing inspiration."

"What do you have to say about rumors that *The Days of Wanting Her Back* is the favorite to win Album of the Year?" one reporter, dressed in a red gown with a mermaid-style skirt, asked Jax.

"I can't possibly comment on that," he said, looking suave as he smiled, raising his scarred brow. "All the nominees are talented—we're happy just to be nominated today."

The funny thing was, unlike most of the people at the award ceremony, he was probably the only one telling the truth. For Jax, going from homeless runaway teenager to rock sensation was plenty. An award on a shelf, he'd told me the week before, would just be a pretty paperweight.

The rest of the band, of course, didn't share his opinion, and neither did I—a win would mean more press, bigger concerts, and the possibility of a music legacy that could last beyond our lifetimes.

As we got to our seats, the enormity of the event really struck me. Here we were, sitting next to actors, musicians, producers . . . all the people who made the industry tick. After weeks of preparing for the awards ceremony, it was really happening.

Once the host, an edgy comedian with a dig about most of the stars in attendance, took the podium and got started with his routine, the only question on my mind was what he'd say about the Hitchcocks. It happened, finally, just before the Best Album nominations were read out, after we'd been sitting politely clapping for winners and nominees for over two hours.

"As for the crowd favorites, the Hitchcocks," the host was saying as the crowd erupted in scattered "wooooo" sounds, "Are they here because of their music or because they've got Khal Drogo leading the band and slaying everyone who gets in their way?"

Jax and I turned to one another laughing—we'd watched all of *Game of Thrones* together, and I had noticed his resemblance to the show's powerful horse lord character more than once.

As the nominees were announced, I gulped, taking a look around. I knew it wasn't the end of the world if The Hitchcocks lost, but by the way their knuckles clenched white around the seat arms, I also knew that every member of the band—even Jax—wanted a win more than anything.

"And the winner of Best Album of the Year goes to. . ." the host said, tearing a side off the envelope and peering at the paper within with a grin as I squeezed Jax's hand.

"The Hitchcocks, with *The Days of Wanting Her Back*!"

Instantly, the auditorium erupted into thunderous applause. Sky's jaw dropped, and Chewie and Kev gave each other a high five as they got up.

I clapped wildly as Jax stood, but then he held his hand out to me.

"Wait, what?" I asked incredulously. I wasn't part of the band—there was no reason for me to be up on stage when they accepted their award.

"Come up there with us," he said, still holding his hand out, with a glint in his eyes I'd never seen before. "Trust me."

My mouth opened to object, but when would I ever get the chance to do this again? I reached up and took his hand, grinning ear to ear, and made my way down the aisle of the auditorium with the rest of the band.

The spotlights shone down on us as we climbed the stairs and Jax took the mic at the podium. "Wow," he said, testing the heft of the statuette in his hand. "So this is how it feels."

From the audience, a female voice shrieked: "WE LOVE YOU, JAX!"

He cleared his throat and took a deep breath. "I want to thank my band, the best band in the world, The Hitchcocks, for being the greatest people I could imagine touring with. My manager, Reed, all the people at our record label . . . but they're not the ones I want to thank most. One person made this entire album possible, and she's standing with us right now. Riley . . . "

He turned to me, and suddenly I felt like the eyes of the entire world were staring in my direction.

"Riley," he started, then noticed that I was looking out at the audience. He looked at me closely, then put two fingers up to his eyes, then toward mine. "Look at me, Pepper. Look at me like it's just the two of us here."

My breath shallow and fast, I turned to look at him. His eyes were deeper, more soulful, than I'd ever seen them.

"Riley, we've been through incredible things together. Amazing ones, terrible ones—and the only constant is that I love you more through every experience we have together." I felt myself blushing in the heat of the light as he spoke, and I could hear the audience start to murmur among themselves. "You're my muse. You're my rock. I want to keep you safe always. I want you by my side forever. Riley . . ."

My heart beat faster and faster as his words sunk in, and then Jax, his voice nearly cracking with emotion, said, "Will you marry me?"

My eyes opened wide, and my hands flew to my mouth. I nodded, trying to get my bearings, and tears started coming to my eyes. "Yes!" I cried out. The audience broke out into whoops and cheers, and a thousand flashes lit up as photos snapped all over the room.

He held out a ring, sparkling in the intense lights. I walked toward the podium, and he slid it around my finger. I looked back to the rest of the band with an incredulous look on my face, as if to ask, *did any of you know about this?* They stared back with sheepish grins. I wondered, grinning, how long this had been part of the plan . . .

and then I felt Jax's lips, kissing me in front of the audience, the cameras, the world. His mouth pressed against mine in a frenzy that shut out anyone but the two of us, locked close together in an embrace no one could tear apart.

I drank the moment in. Life wouldn't always be like this, I knew, and I'd want these memories to last for the rest of my life.

I'd done what no one—including me—had ever thought possible. I'd made the rockstar mine.

The band members stepped over, congratulating us loudly as they hugged us. "Hell yeah, dude," Chewie said, thumping Jax on the back. "Now, let's go celebrate! I've got us VIP invites to every afterparty this town has to offer."

Jax looked at me with his scarred brow raised quizzically, and I smirked at him.

"Thanks for the offer, but I think our afterparty is going to be just the two of us."

Laughing, holding hands, we walked away toward the backstage doors.

It was going to be a good night. And things were only getting better.

**Jax and Riley's story is over for now, but don't miss out on Kristen and Vincent's story in:**

**Forbidden Surrender (The Forever Series)**

Keep reading for an exclusive excerpt!

Thank you for reading!

If you could spare a moment to leave a review it would be much appreciated.

Reviews help new readers find my books! They also provide valuable feedback for my writing!

: )

# Sign up for my mailing list to find out about when I release new books!

http://eepurl.com/sH7wn

## Other books by Priscilla West

Forbidden Surrender (The Forever Series)
Secret Surrender (The Forever Series)
Beautiful Surrender (The Forever Series)
Wrecked (The Forever Series)
Rescued (The Forever Series)
Reckless (The Forever Series)

# Forbidden Surrender (The Forever Series)

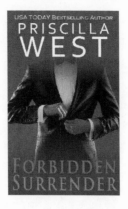

*"What gives you a thrill Kristen?"*

The minute I saw Vincent Sorenson, I knew he was trouble. Arrogant. Possessive. Controlling. He was everything I craved, and nothing I needed.

Unfortunately, I couldn't just avoid him. The higher ups at my company decided they needed his business, and I was on the team to bring him in. Vincent Sorenson didn't seem as interested in business as he was in me, but I knew that was a door better left unopened. If I got involved with him, it would only unearth the pain I spent years trying to bury.

I thought I had it under control, but I seriously underestimated Vincent's seductive charm and silver-tongue. I would soon find out how delicious it would feel to let myself fall into this forbidden surrender.

## An Exclusive Teaser from Forbidden Surrender

When I got back to my hotel room Riley was curled up on the bed watching television. Richard had gone to his own room to do who knows what.

"So how did it go?" Riley paused after I shot her a miserable look. "I'm so sorry, Kris. You don't have to talk about it."

I kicked off my heels and let my hair down, anxious to get out of professional mode. "Richard seems to think we did well. Sometimes I feel like he's in his own world though. Vincent was definitely not going for our pitch. You could totally read it in his body language."

Riley's expression was sympathetic. Remote in her hand, she switched off the TV. "I'm sure you did your best. Maybe luck just wasn't on your side today."

"That's the thing. I couldn't even do my best. I messed up multiple times." My mind replayed the awkward moments from the meeting and I shuddered. I didn't have anyone to blame but myself, but in my current mood I was eager for a scapegoat. "If Vincent wasn't so damn gorgeous, things might've been different."

"Oh, do tell." Her voice increased a pitch.

I told her all about my blunders, and when I was done she smiled. "Well at least you *looked* professional."

"Thanks for the sympathy." I gave her a wry grin.

"You know I'm always here for support. That's why we're going to have a blast today. You're going to forget all about that meeting and Mr. Abs Sorenson. Tonight we'll hit the bars and have guys buy us drinks. I know you haven't been dating much, all that sexual frustration must be eating you alive."

It was true. I'd only gone on a handful of unsuccessful dates since I'd met Riley. I told myself it was because I focusing on my career instead, but there were also personal reasons I didn't want to think about dating—reasons I never told Riley. Still, she was right about the sexual frustration. If my battery-operated boyfriend could talk, he'd probably say I was smothering him.

"I'm not really interested in the male species right now. Between Richard's chauvinism and Vincent shooting us down today, I think I'm a little burned out on testosterone."

"Fair enough. It'll just be us girls then. Get in that sexy bathing suit you brought." Riley untied her robe to reveal her bikini, its thin straps and enhanced bust leaving little to the imagination. "I'm all ready to go."

Having vented to Riley, I felt better about the situation this morning. I slipped into my bathing suit and left the hotel with her.

When we arrived at the aptly-named Bikini Beach just before noon, the shore was packed. There was a nice mix of tourists and locals, with lots of people both in and out of the clear blue waters. We laid our towels down on the heated sand and relaxed in cheap folding chairs we got from a nearby beach store. Once we were settled, Riley went to get us some drinks. I stared out at the waves and thought about how picturesque the scene looked. This kind of experience was rare when you lived in Manhattan and I took the opportunity to soak it in. As the afternoon wore on, the stress of the morning seemed to melt away like the ice cubes in our mojitos.

I spotted a few surfers in the distance zig-zagging along the water. I'd never been surfing before and didn't have much of a desire to change that. I understood the appeal, but I was afraid of the danger—I just didn't think the risks outweighed the benefits. A few thrilling moments versus the possibility of getting my arm bitten off by a shark or getting stung by a jellyfish . . . yeah, I'd be happy with just tanning—with sunscreen of course.

Vincent, on the other hand, loved risky activities. His whole business was based on extreme sports. I didn't really get it but it clearly made him very successful.

A few toned men with olive skin passed by and Riley directed my attention to them. I had to admit they were attractive from a purely physical perspective but that just didn't do it for me.

"Maybe your standards are too high," Riley said.

"Just because they have abs and a penis doesn't mean I want to sleep with them."

She laughed. "Keith had more than that. You never told me why you turned down my offer to set you up with him."

"He just wasn't my type."

"What *is* your type, Kris? I've hardly seen you date since I've known you, and don't say it's because you've been too busy with work." She nudged me with her elbow.

"I'm not sure I have one." I was only vaguely aware of rubbing my own pinky finger.

"Oh come on. Every girl has a type, some just aren't willing to be honest about it."

Now I was the curious one. "What's your type then?"

"Let's see . . . tall, strong, handsome, smart, dark, dangerous . . . oh and let's not forget rich."

"Sounds more like a fantasy than a real person." Actually that sounded a lot like someone I met this morning. "Why don't we just say I like the 'nice and caring' type."

"Basically boring then, huh?"

"Boring to you, satisfying to me. Why would you want someone dark and dangerous? And if he's so hot, wouldn't you be concerned he'd cheat on you?"

"I'd just have to blow his mind." Her mischievous wink made it clear what she meant. "But to each her own."

We spent the rest of the afternoon bathing our skin in UV rays and trying out the local food. Fortunately, there were enough tourists streaming through Cape Town that the restaurants provided menus in English. I thought chicken would taste the same no matter where you were but whatever special sauce they used made it exceptionally delicious. We explored the area, stopping periodically to point out unique architecture or unusual occurrences. Although I'd told Riley I wasn't interested in dating, I couldn't help but indulge in idle thoughts about Vincent. Maybe I'd spent way too much time memorizing his files.

It was evening by the time we were hungry again. Despite wearing comfy sneakers, our feet were killing us from all the walking. Riley suggested we rest at a local bar to relieve our weary legs and grab some grub. We were off the beaten path by this point and the bar she picked looked sketchy.

"It'll be fun. Don't you want to get an authentic experience? We didn't fly thousands of miles just to go to some bar we could go to back home."

"Yeah, but we're two American girls in a foreign country. There are horror movies based on this situation."

"What's the worst that can happen?" Her grin made me ill at ease.

"Don't say that."

"Look, I have some mace in my bag. If anybody tries to get frisky with us, I'm going to melt their eyeballs." I pictured Riley as the female version of Rambo.

"All right, fine. If we get abducted, it's your fault. I just don't want you saying I'm a party pooper."

She laughed. "I've never said that. You just like to be cautious, which I respect. Remember when you warned me about Danny? You were right, he did turn out to be a creep."

Riley had dated Danny a few months prior. When she brought him over to our apartment he kept giving me shifty-eyed stares. I expressed my concerns to her and it turned out he had done time in prison for theft. He wasn't even the worst of Riley's extensive dating history. I honestly didn't know how she found some of these guys.

Upon entering, we found the place was full of mostly locals. There were a few expats in the corner who sounded British and were probably out for some adventure. Somewhere there was a speaker putting out exotic tribal music. The hypnotic beats were catchy but it certainly was a far cry from American pop music—no Miley Cyrus here. When we found a seat at a table and ordered margaritas, I found myself easing into the atmosphere.

"Man, check this place out." Riley sounded excited. She pointed at the decorations around us. "Animal bones hanging on the walls, a shrunken head behind the bar, and a beat-up sign that says 'Ompad'. Isn't it cool?" She whipped out her phone to snap some pictures.

The distinct sound of a shot glass slamming against wood alerted us to a commotion brewing near the bar. A group of onlookers surrounded two men with tumblers in hand and a bottle half-full of amber liquid between them. The one on the left was a juggernaut of a man; a gruff beard and mean stare completed the intimidation factor. The gathering of curious spectators obscured my view of the man on the right.

"What's going on over there?" Riley asked.

I knew we shouldn't have gotten closer. The feeling in my gut that whatever was going on over there was trouble told me we should leave, but intense curiosity pulled us near the action like moths to a flame.

We settled at a table nearby, giving us front row seats. It was when I saw who the figure poised on the right was that I realized why my alarm bells had gone off.

*Vincent.*

What was he doing here? He was wearing a white button-down and khakis that showcased his lean muscular build. By now the crowd around the bar had grown considerably, tantamount with the noise level. Most huddled around Vincent's side. Some of the admirers included beautiful, curvaceous women that were all but rubbing their breasts against Vincent, and a pang of jealousy hit me from who knows where.

Riley shouted to me over the ruckus. "Is that who I think it is?"

"Yeah, it's Vincent," I said. "Looks like he's in the middle of some kind of drinking game."

I couldn't hear her response over the cheering. The only two words I managed to decipher were "fucking" and "hot."

I leaned in closer to her. "I can't hear you."

"I said you should go over there. This could be your second chance to win him over."

"What? I don't even know what he's doing. He might not even remember me."

"You pinched his goddamn nipple, of course he'll remember you. Go find out." She nudged my shoulder but I remained steadfast in my seat. As serendipitous as this encounter was, I wasn't comfortable with the idea of approaching Vincent in this strange social situation. If Richard had been right about the meeting going well, talking to Vincent could sabotage our efforts rather than help.

"Let's just watch them a little first."

We witnessed the burly guy down his shot, slam his glass against the counter, and grunt something in Afrikaans. I couldn't understand it, but if I had to guess by the tone, it meant "Is that the best you got?" He then reached into a nearby bag sitting on the counter and produced a large clear jar. I squinted my eyes to identify the contents. Thin strands, black dots scurrying.

*Cobwebs and spiders.*

The crowd didn't seem surprised, instead they clamored approval like they were at a sporting event. Why would he have such a thing? And here of all places. *I hate spiders.*

My disgust and surprise must have been palpable because Vincent turned his head in my direction as if attuned to my specific frequency. For the second time today, we locked eyes. A part of me wanted to hide from the embarrassment of this morning, another part of me knew my company had important business to conduct with him.

Before I decided whether I was going to wave at him or shrink behind the crowd of bodies, a ghost of a smile touched his lips.

He waved me over. In disbelief, I pointed my finger at my chest as I mouthed "me?" and he nodded. What did he want with me? I looked to Riley for advice and was met with eager shooing motions. Sensing an opportunity to clear up any confusion over this morning's meeting, I worked my way through the crowd to him. The women around him were reluctant to make room, shooting me catty-glares, but I managed to wiggle through an opening.

"Hello Kristen," he said.

He did remember my name. "Hello Mr. Sorenson."

"Please, just call me Vincent. I didn't expect to see you here, but now that you are, this'll be a lot more interesting." He grinned.

I wasn't sure what he meant. Confused by the whole situation, I asked, "What are you doing here, Vincent?"

"Business. And you're going to decide if you want to help me." He gestured to the big guy and his bizarre pet spiders.

*Okay . . . that doesn't explain a whole lot.*

"I should tell you, Mr. Sorenson. I have a fear of spiders," I said, eyeing the jar.

He leaned close to my ear so I could hear him. "All the better. You asked for my money earlier today, Kristen." His smoky voice was implacable. "I wasn't impressed. Here's your second chance to convince me to trust you with my assets."

*Shit.* We *did* blow the meeting this morning. I gulped. "What do you want me to do?"

As if to answer my question, the hulk uncapped the jar and picked out a spider with a pair of chopsticks.

The sight of the tiny black creature outside its confines made me panic. I tried to escape but Vincent caught my elbow in a light but secure grip and pulled me to him. "You're fine, trust me. Just watch."

With his hand on the filled shot glass, the big guy placed the spider on the skin between his thumb and forefinger. The spider—whose backside displayed a red dot—remained surprisingly still, perhaps in as much suspense as I was. Never taking his eyes off the poisonous creature, the big guy slowly brought the drink to his lips, keeping his hand steady, and in one smooth motion downed the contents, flicked the spider off his hand, and crushed the arachnid as he slammed his glass on the bar. The crowd erupted in cheers.

The big guy looked expectantly at me and Vincent. His steely eyes said "your turn".

"You're not seriously going to do that are you?" I blurted without thinking.

His eyes narrowed as he smiled. "I am. And you're going to help me by putting the spider on my hand."

I was about to say "hell no" but thought better when I noticed his probing eyes. "I'm really not comfortable with this."

"Consider it a test. How far are you willing to go to serve my interests?"

I felt my breaths shorten. "Are we talking about money here or poisonous spiders? Because those are two very different things."

"Believe it or not, there's a lot at stake if I don't follow through." He gestured to a pile of documents on the counter. I couldn't read the language, but from the formatting I could tell they were contract documents—so this wasn't just a wager between two inflated egos. "I imagine there's also a lot at stake for you."

"What if it bites you?"

"Let me worry about that. If it does, it won't be your fault."

"What if it climbs up and bites me?"

"I won't let it happen. Trust me, you'll be fine."

This wasn't professional; this was insane. Crazy. I'd never done anything close to this dangerous before. If I had known I'd have to handle deadly bugs to win clients, I might not have taken this job in the first place.

I was stuck between a rock and a hard place: don't do it and for sure lose Vincent as a client; do it and possibly kill both the hottest man I'd ever met and my career. Either way, I was screwed.

I glanced over at Riley and saw her give me a thumbs up.

*Damn you, Vincent.* I picked up the chopsticks and unscrewed the jar, grimacing as I lowered the utensil inside.

When I touched one of the creatures, it moved and I instinctively retracted my hand.

"No way. I can't do this," I exclaimed.

"Giving up so soon? Nothing worth pursuing comes without risk."

Inflamed by his taunting, I tried again. This time the black creature didn't move and I was able to clamp it with the chopsticks. It felt hard and squishy at the same time and when I pulled it out and got a better view of its wriggling legs, it took every ounce of willpower not to throw it across the bar. My hands were trembling and I was afraid I'd drop the spider or worse, rile it up enough to bite Vincent. Then a warm hand around my upper arm steadied me.

"You're doing great. Just relax a little. Focus on controlling your own body, not on what you're holding."

"Easier said than done," I replied, even though his advice seemed to be working.

The next few moments were a blur, but I somehow managed to place the spider gently on Vincent's hand. He downed his drink and went the extra mile by flicking the spider back into the jar instead of killing it.

Once again, the bar roared approval.

Afraid I would have to do it again, I turned to the big guy and was relieved to see him passed out on the counter.

Vincent had won.


It wasn't long before the ruckus died down. The big guy had woken up, signed the contract, shook Vincent's hand, and left. The crowd had dissipated and Riley was now being entertained by one of the British guys from the expat group. I found myself seated beside Vincent at a cozy table in a secluded part of the bar, alone.

Even with all the alcohol I imagined was flowing through his system, Vincent looked as sober as a judge. Not only were his nerves steel, but so was his blood. I began to wonder if those were the only parts . . .

"What can I get you to drink?" Vincent asked, flagging the waitress.

I considered avoiding more alcohol in case we discussed business, but I didn't want to be rude either. "A mojito please."

The waitress flashed a flirty smile at Vincent before leaving, which made me bristle.

He returned his attention back to me. "I'm surprised. You struck me as more damsel than dame."

The comment was decidedly personal and I felt justified in taking offense. "And you strike me as more reckless than brave. Why were you in a drinking contest with a spider-loving thug?"

His sinful lips curved into a wicked smile. "You can't always judge people by their appearance. Nambe is a real estate mogul. He owns a lot of property in the area including this bar. I wanted one of his private beaches and he set the terms. You'll find the most successful people play by their own rules."

His comment made me recall how far I had just gone to win him over as a client. "Do all your business transactions involve endangering your life?"

"Just the interesting ones. The bite wouldn't have been fatal if I went to the hospital immediately. When you want something bad enough, sometimes it's surprising what you're willing to do." He adjusted his seat and his leg brushed mine sending an unwelcome flutter through my belly.

The waitress returned with my drink and I took a sip, relishing the taste more than I should have. "Does that apply to swimming with sharks and jumping off cliffs?" I said, feeling emboldened by the mojito as well as the other alcoholic beverages I'd consumed since setting foot inside this bar.

"It applies to whatever gives me a thrill. What gives you a thrill Kristen? Besides winning my account."

Unsure if that was a flirtatious line or an accusation, I answered, "Who says that gives me a thrill?"

"It makes you good at your job. Pitch aside, the materials you gave me were polished."

"Thank you." I flustered at the compliment. It was rare to have my work given the appreciation I felt it deserved even by my colleagues, let alone a client.

"What would you do if I chose your company?"

"You're saying after I did all that, you're still not convinced you can trust us with your money?"

"What you did puts Waterbridge-Howser back in the running. After your partner insulted my intelligence this morning I had almost ruled you out."

*Crap.* "I'm truly sorry about that, it wasn't intentional. We were just trying to be persuasive and it seems we missed the mark."

"Fair enough." He stirred his drink and shrugged. "I'm curious, what are you doing in a bar like this?"

The question sounded like he thought I was here on the prowl—which was not at all the reason. "It was my friend Riley's idea." I pointed a blaming finger at Riley across the bar, who seemed to be too enamored with her company to notice. "She's a little adventurous."

"So are you," he said touching my hand with the tip of his finger. "Do you have a boyfriend?"

"Excuse me?" The conversation had turned decidedly flirtatious and I wasn't sure how to react. I'd never been hit on by a potential client before and there were no company guidelines addressing this type of situation. Regardless of how attracted I was to Vincent, if anybody at work suspected I was mixing business with pleasure, my professional reputation would be ruined. I'd seen it happen before.

"Don't tell me your partner is."

"You mean Richard? He's definitely *not* my boyfriend."

"Good. So you're single." He leaned his breathtaking face closer to mine heightening awareness of him.

I stood my ground. "Maybe I am, maybe I'm not. Either way I'm sorry to disappoint you, but I don't date potential clients," I said, hoping the brush-off would end the personal discussion and we could return to talking about business.

Those seductive lips so close to mine curved into a smile. "Who says anything about dating? I just want to finish what you started this morning."

"What are you talking about?"

"We were here." He gently but firmly took my hand in his and placed it on his chest. The move caught me off guard and all I could do was suck in a deep breath when I felt the sudden warmth of his body and the strong beat of his heart beneath my palms. "Let's move it further." He began to move my hand slowly downward. As my fingertips traced the hard contours at the base of his pecs and the firm cut of his stomach through his shirt, goosebumps ran across my skin and the hairs on the back of my neck stiffened. My pulse quickened and my lips parted to accommodate faster breaths. It wasn't until my fingers reached the base of his stony abs that my mind caught up and I pulled away.

"This morning was an innocent mistake," I shot back, aware I was more aroused than offended by the gesture. "I don't know what kind of girl you think I am exactly, but I don't mix business with pleasure."

"I do." His sexy voice could tear down any woman's defenses. I knew I had to get away, afraid I wouldn't be an exception.

"Good for you. Thank you for the drink Mr. Sorenson but if you'll excuse me, I need to get back to my friend." I rose from my seat with the intention of leaving but turned back to that gorgeous face one last time. "If you're still interested in Waterbridge-Howser, you have Richard's number."

His lips curled into that same wicked smile from earlier. "We'll be in touch."